The Strangest Thing

A Brian Sadler Archaeological Mystery

by
Bill Thompson

Oscar + Kathy —
Hope you enjoy this book —
Thank you for your friendship
Bill Thompson
5.16.14.

Published by
Ascendente Books

Published by Ascendente Books

ISBN 978-1495494017

Printed in the United States of America

Books by Bill Thompson

<u>Brian Sadler Archaeological Mystery Series</u>

THE BETHLEHEM SCROLL

**ANCIENT: A SEARCH FOR THE LOST CITY
OF THE MAYAS**

THE STRANGEST THING

<u>Teen fiction</u>

THE LEGEND OF GUNNERS COVE

DEDICATION

I want to mention three people who've accompanied
me on trips to strange and unusual places.

First there are my two sons, Jeff and Ryan Thompson.
With them I have seen wonderful things - the Nazca
lines, Sacsayhuaman and Machu Picchu in Peru and the
marvels of Egypt.

My good friend David Crocker was with us in Peru.
Later I made another trip to Egypt and also to Petra
with him and his family.

And it was David who was with me the first time I saw
the Temple of the Inscriptions at Palenque, the subject
of *The Strangest Thing*.

To these three companions in adventure
I dedicate this book.

THE STRANGEST THING

"HAVE NO FEAR OF THEM
FOR NOTHING IS COVERED THAT WILL NOT BE
REVEALED,
OR HIDDEN THAT WILL NOT BE KNOWN."

MATTHEW 10:26

BILL THOMPSON

HISTORICAL PRELUDE
Palenque and the Tomb of King Pakal

The ancient Mayan city of Palenque lies in a heavily forested area in the state of Chiapas, Mexico, close to the Guatemalan border. Fifteen hundred years ago the great Maya civilization stretched from east central Mexico southwards through what is now Guatemala, Belize and Honduras. Today the area around Palenque – in fact the entire state of Chiapas - has a certain wild-west flair. The state previously was part of Guatemala and seems so different from the rest of Mexico that many residents believe Chiapas should be that way again. Rebels wearing ski masks and toting automatic rifles are visible evidence of the support of these people for secession from Mexico. They run crude checkpoints along the highways of Chiapas, blocking the road with vehicles and even tanks they have "appropriated" from the Government. Although fearsome in appearance they pose no real threat to the tourists who make their ways to the old Mayan city.

There is no Maya site about which more is known than Palenque. It was on the radar of explorers, raiders and archaeologists two hundred years ago. It is the archetypical lost city – hidden in the dense forest for a millennium before being located by pioneer exploration teams who marveled at its skyscraper temples. Never mind that these men thought Palenque had been built by Egyptians. Its grandeur and sheer size gave them little reason to believe the truth: it was built by the Mayan people. How an unsophisticated band of people in the jungles of Central America learned architecture, symmetry, the raising of multi-ton stones a hundred feet high – construction techniques that are difficult even today – has always been puzzling. They emerged from farming and warring to building hundreds of massive structures. These buildings were built over a thousand-mile area in what are now Honduras, Guatemala, Belize and Mexico. And they went from being farmers to becoming master architects in less than three generations.

How did they do this? Were they taught? If so, by whom? How and where did they get the knowledge to build these massive structures all over Central America?

Even in today's partially excavated state, the city of Palenque is reminiscent of the power and authority of its rulers. Significant inscriptions have been discovered that have aided scholars in understanding the Maya civilization. And the site itself is breathtaking – ancient skyscraper temples reach toward the heavens while tall mounds nearby promise more to come once funds and time to excavate become available. As university archaeological expeditions open buildings heretofore covered in trees and dirt, they find exciting new things. In the 1990s, for instance, the South Group of buildings was excavated, resulting in some impressive and spectacular discoveries including rare examples of Mayan writing.

Mostly restored, the so-called Temple of the Inscriptions is considered one of the finest examples of Mayan architecture and Palenque's most striking structure. It was built during the reign of King K'inich Janaab Pakal (Pakal the Great) who lived from 603 to 683 AD.

In 1952 Alberto Ruz, the director of research at Mexico's National Institute of Anthropology and History, discovered the answer to a question that had long puzzled archaeologists about the Temple of the Inscriptions. There were several holes drilled through a stone that lay in the middle of the temple's top floor, many stories above the verdant jungle below. No one knew why the holes were there until Ruz and a team of men dug far below the floor and shined a light through a small hole his men had cut into the limestone below. He looked upon a room he described as a "vision from a fairy tale . . . a magic grotto . . . an abandoned chapel." When he gazed downwards, he saw something that had not been seen by human eyes in over a thousand years – the magnificent carved lid of the sarcophagus of a person who had to have been a very important ruler. In fact, the immense Temple of the Inscriptions had been built over and around the tomb.

Today travelers to Palenque are offered the opportunity to see the room where the ruler still rests. It lies deep within the pyramid; to get there one must start from the very top of the pyramid, snake his way down a stone staircase in a narrow passage that winds down seventy-five feet through the middle of the temple. It is no place for those suffering from claustrophobia - the air quickly becomes stale and close. Maneuvering the passage is like crawling through a small opening in a cave. It's not for the faint of heart.

At last the passageway opens into a crypt constructed below the base of the temple at the time the pyramid was built. Inside the room is the intact resting place of a man ultimately identified as King Pakal, ruler of Palenque at the height of its power and prestige and the builder of the Temple of the Inscriptions.

The elaborate lid of Pakal's sarcophagus is an enigma. It is covered with ornate and very peculiar drawings and is one of the great mysteries of modern times. Many archaeologists believe it shows the King dying like the setting sun, journeying into the underworld of death and emerging as the rising sun. But ancient astronaut theorists and many others claim it clearly shows the king in some type of space vehicle, his hand on a lever and his body lying back as if preparing to be launched in a rocket. If you look at the drawings on the lid with an open mind you can see how the latter viewpoint arose.

In every Mayan city archaeologists have found that temples and pyramids were constructed on top of and/or surrounding earlier structures. Many rulers chose to enhance, beautify and expand existing buildings rather than starting from scratch.

Although there is no historical evidence that this was the case at the monument called the Temple of the Inscriptions where King Pakal was buried, this book offers the premise that this particular temple at Palenque, like countless other buildings in ancient Mayan cities, was itself constructed around and atop something far, far older than the Maya civilization – perhaps even older than civilization itself.

CHAPTER ONE

Tuesday

Two days before the disappearance

President John Chapman was stretched out on a couch in front of a roaring fire in the Oval Office of the White House. He had kicked off his shoes and grabbed a rare half hour of solitude between meetings. In his hand was the latest issue of Archaeology Magazine. He was deeply engrossed in an article about a recent find - a hidden city in Peru, one that could rival Machu Picchu in size and grandeur once it was excavated.

Chapman had a passion for archaeological adventure. He loved the reports of new discoveries and enjoyed reading about expeditions to remote areas in virtually impenetrable jungles. As the most powerful man on earth, he was privy to the newest and latest things people were finding worldwide. He fueled his hobby by making sure his contacts around the world kept him informed of interesting developments in their countries.

The President was a scion of one of America's wealthiest families. Other men of vast wealth had been elected President, most recently John F. Kennedy, whose net worth in today's dollars was estimated at over $1 billion. George Washington, the father of our country, was second on the most-wealthy list at around $500 million. Chapman didn't hold a candle to those two but he was worth well over $250 million personally.

Men such as John Chapman instantly got what they wanted and needed. Chapman had never done the things others take for granted, like waiting in line or being put on hold for three minutes or being denied the best table at a restaurant. At this lofty level of power some people tend to be curt and impatient with others. John Chapman was one of those. He could be the friendliest guy in the world at a baby-kissing political fund-raiser. Touring a factory, you'd think he empathized totally with the people pushing brooms or installing widgets.

But he didn't. People who have the influence and money of John Chapman's family think differently than the rest of us. They *were* different, of course, with all that power. But a few of them, like President Chapman's parents, instilled in their children the notion that they were better than other people – that the have-nots were there to serve the ones with money. Families like this would have been happy in eighteenth century England where the wealthy owned the land and cast the votes while the uneducated poor were their indentured servants.

Interestingly, many of these people were never satisfied with what they had. They wanted more. More power. More money. More excitement. More first-hand looks at the rarest, strangest and newest discoveries in the world.

President Chapman had forty-eight hours left.

A quiet ding across the room took him away from the Andes Mountains and back to reality. He went to his desk, glanced quickly at his computer screen to see whose call had been sent through, then picked up the phone and spoke to the Vice President, William Henry Harrison IV.

The President skipped the pleasantries. "Harry, the Senate has to pass that pipeline bill. It's been held up in committee for weeks and I'm surprised your constituents in Oklahoma aren't yelling their heads off. The pipeline from Canada to south Texas benefits everyone. My Nebraska friends certainly want to see it happen and I know your people do too. So get in there and twist a few arms. Get this bill out of committee and on the floor. Then get it passed!" Chapman listened a moment then abruptly hung up. He got Harry Harrison's word that the bill would be brought out and successfully dealt with. Harry had never let John Chapman down. And Chapman knew he wouldn't do it now. People who let him down usually lived to regret it.

THE STRANGEST THING

Another ding alerted him to look at the monitor on the credenza behind his desk. His personal secretary, one of three at his disposal, advised him the U.S. Ambassador to Mexico was on the phone. Few calls received Chapman's immediate attention - those from a select group were the exception. It was possible this was a business call but Chapman hoped it wasn't. His adrenalin always began flowing when he anticipated the possibility that someone was calling to give him inside news about his passionate hobby.

Picking up the receiver, President Chapman said, "Good morning, Mr. Ambassador. I hope things are well with you down in Mexico City." The President glanced at his computer screen. "How's Elizabeth and how are Paul and Kevin?"

Each time John Chapman's private secretary sent through a call she accompanied it with an instant message providing information about the person who was on the line. These notes always included names of spouses and children, including their ages. If Chapman had been with the caller in the past year, that notation was included as well so he could easily and simply refer to their last meeting as though it were fresh on his mind. That was a big help for President Chapman since his lack of concern for other people was well known inside the White House but a secret to most outsiders.

"My family and I are fine, Mr. President. Thank you for asking. I know your time is valuable so let me get right to the purpose of my call. The last time you and I were together you spoke of your passion for archaeology

11

and ancient enigmas. I took the liberty of letting a couple of friends know of your interest. They run the archaeological side of things at the National Institute here in Mexico City. I told them I'd consider it a personal favor if I could be among the first to know if anything new and unusual turned up. And this one involves Palenque – a place you already know about.

"Remember the phone call you made a couple of months ago to smooth the process for Sussex University to get its dig permits at Palenque? That allowed their team to get started much faster than usual. They've been working there awhile. No one knew if anything else might be found buried there along with King Pakal's body. But sir, they've really come across something unique. I think you're going to want to see it."

John Chapman felt excitement growing inside as he listened to the Ambassador describe an incredible, almost unbelievable discovery at Palenque in the southernmost Mexican state of Chiapas. The Ambassador stated that the find had so far not been disclosed to the public. Chapman knew that was true – if this information were available to anyone on earth he would have known already.

"In case you wanted to see what they've found, sir," the Ambassador said, "I've arranged to have everything put on hold for a couple of days. It took some doing - I called in a favor. A team of archaeological students from Sussex University has been excavating in the area for over a year. It doesn't hurt that Sussex is my alma mater – in fact the current president of the

12

university and I were fraternity brothers there. I don't know if your schedule permits a quick trip but I thought you would want to know regardless."

The President had to see this for himself. "I'm really glad you called me, Mr. Ambassador. I'm truly fascinated by what I've heard from you today. I took a look at my calendar while we were talking - I can be there day after tomorrow. How do you suggest we arrange things logistically?"

"I was thinking that through, sir. If you don't mind flying under the radar, so to speak, I think it would be better to avoid publicity and questions both here and in the USA. If you can fly to Palenque I'll meet you and escort you by private car to the ruins; it'll take less than a half hour to get there. Then we can visit the discovery site itself. Will you spend the night?"

"I'll be there early on Thursday morning and I'll need to do it all in one day. It's a lot easier that way anyway. I'll have my assistant call with all the details in the morning and we'll bring the Gulfstream if the Palenque airport's big enough."

"Given your circumstances I certainly understand that it's easier to go back instead of staying, Mr. President. And the airport can accommodate a Gulfstream. I'll wait for the call tomorrow and I'll be at the airport in Palenque Thursday when you arrive. There's not much at the airport so don't be surprised at how basic things are." The conversation was ended.

John Chapman sat back in his chair, hands entwined behind his head. He reflected on the good fortune he had in being who he was. He could be first at anything he wanted and this time he was going to be one of the first to see what undoubtedly would be the most extraordinary discovery he had ever come across. He pressed a button; within seconds a door opened and his appointments secretary came into the room.

"Sit down, Nancy. I need to change my plans for the day after tomorrow."

She glanced at an iPad in her lap. "But sir, the Prime Minister of Israel is set . . ."

His response was curt. "I don't care. Cancel everything and book what I tell you."

CHAPTER TWO

Two hours later John Chapman's appointments secretary had completed the change in plans the President had outlined and she had passed details about the upcoming trip both to his personal secretary and the head of security. Her part was over – a Gulfstream G650 jet would be standing by to take Chapman and two Secret Service agents to Palenque. Everyone knew times and places, enough for the pilot to file a flight plan. It wasn't the large plane Chapman normally used; this one was small and unobtrusive – exactly what was needed for this particular trip.

His calendar, previously full of appointments on Thursday, now only showed the words "personal time" to anyone who was high enough in the organization to access it. And his public calendar, the one that was posted online for the world to see, still showed a full, normal day, with one Senator, school group or awards ceremony after another parading through the President's office and taking up his time. Only a handful, those who knew Chapman's real plans, was aware these meetings were all fictitious.

Personal secretary Bridget Malone looked at the itinerary the appointments secretary had emailed. In large letters at the top were the words "TOP SECRET." She read through it and shook her head. *He's off on another of his wild goose chases,* she thought. *As busy as he is, why he makes time for this stuff is beyond me.* But she also had known Chapman for a long time – she had been part of his staff for nearly twenty years and if she knew anything about him, she knew how passionate he was about ancient things. He had been on expeditions to a remote area of Turkey to view a ruined city perhaps ten thousand years old; he had crawled headfirst down a very narrow passage in a Bolivian pyramid to see a previously undiscovered tomb; he had sat atop a temple in a Guatemalan jungle at midnight to experience the solitude.

John Chapman had a burning desire for adventure. He had little time to read for pleasure anymore but when he did he invariably picked up books asking who built the Sphinx or why the Nazca lines were created thousands of years ago, visible only from the air. He thrived on enigmas. He read about ancient aliens. He devoured books about how old mankind might actually be. And all of his reading material was in hard copy format - he eschewed Kindles, preferring a book you could hold in your hands.

THE STRANGEST THING

Bridget knew what he read because his account at Amazon.com was in her name with shipments delivered to a post office box a few miles from the White House. Once his orders cleared the White House mailroom and were scanned by the Secret Service they were brought unopened to her. It was best that way. People might find it unusual that the United States President was interested in strange, weird subjects. The books never stayed in Chapman's office where others might see them. They went straight to his bedroom bookcase. And so around the office it was a poorly kept secret that John Chapman was an adventurer, a man who probably should have been born as an explorer a hundred years earlier, a man who would drop even the most important appointment to travel two thousand miles to see a discovery. She had no idea this adventure would be different. Less than forty-eight hours remained for what was up to now John Chapman's normal existence.

Looking over his itinerary she saw that Chapman had instructed only two of his Secret Service bodyguards accompany him. Normally there would be at least one more, especially with his heading to an unsettled place like rural Mexico, but his orders would be followed. After all, it was a one-day trip and the way it was being handled less than twenty people would ever know he had been away from the office. Even though they always existed, the chances for problems on this brief excursion were pretty remote.

At four a.m. on Thursday, the day he would disappear, John Chapman heard a light knock on his bedroom door. The President acknowledged he was awake, turned on the light and headed to the bathroom. There was no need to worry about waking Marianne. They hadn't slept in the same bed for over five years, ever since another of John Chapman's dalliances with a young staffer had made the news. This one had been the latest in a string of girls, promises never to do it again, half-hearted pleas for forgiveness.

But this one had been different. This was John Chapman's first affair while President, and this time he didn't plead or promise. He had looked at his wife coldly and said, "If you don't like it, get out. File for divorce. Leave me and this life you have. You're nobody, Marianne. You're a little girl from Omaha and you're nothing without me. You know it and I know it. And we both know you aren't going anywhere. So get over it." He had walked out of the room and slammed the door.

She had drowned her sorrow in several Bourbon and waters that evening after moving her things to a bedroom next door to his. Marianne Chapman hated herself because her husband was right. She stayed for exactly the reasons he had said she'd stay. She craved the attention that came with being First Lady and she didn't want to go back to her old life. But from that day on there was no love, no passion, no hand-holding - except in public, of course. Their marriage of convenience was a well-kept secret. Only the staff of the personal residence within the White House knew they slept in separate rooms, and most of them thought it was because of

THE STRANGEST THING

Chapman's propensity to read books until the wee hours. The First Couple weren't particularly lovey to each other in front of the staff, but they never fought either. They just seemed like an old married couple that had slipped into a bit of complacency.

President Chapman left the White House at 5:15 a.m. He read the morning paper in the rear seat of a black sedan, one bodyguard in the front seat and the other riding in an identical sedan in front of Chapman's car. SUVs flanked the front and rear of the motorcade. The President was dressed in jeans and a golf shirt and wore a light jacket and a Panama hat. His driver had never seen Chapman dress so casually before. With light early morning traffic the sedan pulled up at Andrews Air Force Base just before six o'clock.

"Good morning, sir," a businesslike flight attendant said as Chapman and his two Secret Service agents boarded the Gulfstream G650, newest in the Government's fleet of planes used to shuttle the President around. Considered the world's fastest private aircraft, the plane could fly over six hundred miles per hour and go nonstop from New York to mainland China. Although the standard G650 could seat up to eighteen people, this one had been dramatically modified to carry a maximum of eight passengers while ensuring the comfort and safety of just one – the President of the United States. The aircraft was equipped with a full kitchen and bar and included a stateroom and private bath at the rear of the plane. A flat screen TV mounted on the wall at the front of the cabin was tuned to CNN. The morning news quietly droned in the background. There were no

19

breaking stories of interest to Chapman. That was a good thing since he was heading to the boondocks for the day.

Ordinarily whatever aircraft carried the President automatically used the call sign "Air Force One." Due to the secrecy of this trip Chapman had requested the Gulfstream use its normal tail number instead. Otherwise anyone with the interest and technological savvy could have immediately determined that President Chapman was flying to Palenque.

There were two pilots – the one flying left seat came out of the cockpit and gave John Chapman a briefing. The flight would take a little less than four hours and the trip was scheduled to be smooth and easy. With the time change they should arrive by 9:30 a.m. local time. As the plane taxied to the runway and streaked into the morning sky Chapman settled into his plush seat and opened a black briefcase that had been set at his feet by one of the bodyguards. He retrieved a series of folders and began to peruse their contents one by one. Making notes here and there he found it difficult to concentrate on the work of the nation he governed. His mind continually wandered to the mystery and adventure awaiting him in Palenque, Mexico.

For President John Chapman the real mystery would begin in just a matter of hours.

CHAPTER THREE

Thursday

The day of the disappearance

As the Gulfstream landed a small band of dirty, barefoot children ran across a dusty road to the airstrip to look at the gleaming white airplane. When it came to a stop in front of a shack that was the operations center for the tiny Palenque airport, the kids crowded around the door. Steps were lowered and the two Secret Service agents disembarked. John Chapman stayed inside until a black Lincoln Navigator drew close to the plane. The SUV looked new and had diplomatic license plates, two giveaways that this vehicle wasn't the usual mode of transportation in the sleepy Mexican town.

One of the security people stuck his head back into the cabin and said, "We can go now, sir." Chapman came down the stairs as the bodyguards pushed the children back. No one noticed a raggedy boy reach into his pocket and pull out a cellphone. He pressed a single number, hit "send" and turned the phone off. His job was done and he had earned twenty pesos, about a dollar and fifty cents.

Ignoring the waving children, Chapman strode to the SUV as the front passenger door opened and the U.S. Ambassador to Mexico stepped out. "Good morning, sir!" he said jubilantly to the President. "Are you ready for some adventure?"

"I've thought of virtually nothing else since I spoke with you. Have you heard anything more about the discovery?"

"Nobody's saying anything at this point, which means they're following my request. I'm really happy to report I've heard nothing. Of course there have been guards posted at the site since the discovery was made and the Temple of the Inscriptions has been closed to the public for the last couple of days."

One of Chapman's bodyguards climbed into the front seat of the Navigator while Chapman and the Ambassador sat in the middle row. The other Secret Service agent was in the rear third row. The driver was a young Army captain who turned and said, "I'm pleased to meet you, Mr. President, and pleased to be assisting you today." He pulled away, left the airport and traveled down a two-lane asphalt road.

THE STRANGEST THING

Chapman ignored the driver, turned to the Ambassador and said, "What are the archaeologists telling the public is the reason the temple's closed?"

"They put out a story that there's a flaw in the structural integrity of the passageway leading to King Pakal's tomb. They promised it'd be reopened once repairs are made. Everything's on hold until your visit is over and a decision is made on how to announce the discovery. Sussex University and the patron who funded the exploration of the tomb are involved in all the decisions in tandem with the Mexican archaeological authorities. Even if they reopen the temple, I'm sure they'll continue to keep the descending stairway and Pakal's tomb closed for the time being, given the highly unusual nature of what's been found.

CHAPTER FOUR

As the President landed in Palenque Thomas Newton Torrance enjoyed the view from his desk. Through floor to ceiling panels of glass TNT, as the press had scathingly dubbed him, surveyed the skyscrapers of Manhattan while speaking on the phone, a noontime glass of wine close at hand. Torrance's New York apartment served as his headquarters while he was in the States. The rent on the two thousand square foot flat on East 61st Street was more than at his London home, but neither cost mattered to TNT. One or more of the various companies he controlled paid the rents. Sometimes when things got a little dicey TNT had to move for a time but at the moment things were going fine.

The forty-year-old Torrance had been born in east London. Growing up was tough. The death of his father when the boy was four caused his mother to have to work two jobs and there was never enough of anything.

THE STRANGEST THING

It turned out he had an entrepreneurial flair – at age twelve he organized a few friends and started an exterior housecleaning service that happened to be the right thing at the right time. Within a couple of years it attracted the attention of the local media. Thomas Torrance's business skyrocketed because of the publicity about this teenager's flair for entrepreneurship.

He sold that company for nearly a million dollars when he was only sixteen. He caught the attention of a wealthy businessman who offered him a job scouting venture capital deals in London. The man wanted to locate small companies to buy on the cheap, build up and sell. But Thomas Newton Torrance had a better idea. Why not buy small companies that are publicly traded, he thought. In the days before computer programs would have saved untold time, he spent day after day poring through public documents filed by small companies, looking not for good earnings or good prospects, but for cash reserves.

The first company he found was a business that sold wholesale pool chemicals in Leeds. Its customers were the stores that homeowners visited to buy chlorine and supplies. The firm was a fifty-year-old business and the chairman was nearly seventy. Most important to Torrance was nearly £10 million in cash that the company had accumulated over the years.

Torrance took the deal to his mentor who recognized the boy's talent for deals and was willing to help him become a success. Thomas Torrance had calculated that anyone owning 45% of the company would have effective control – no other single shareholder owned more than 9% and there were so many that it was almost incomprehensible that 51% of them would ever vote together as a block. Thomas' mentor used £2 million of his money to purchase the 45% stake, then gave a half interest in it to Thomas in exchange for a promissory note to repay it in twelve months. Thomas asked his mentor what would happen if he couldn't repay the money that quickly. The man smiled and assured Thomas there would be no problems. They both knew exactly what the game plan was going to be and where the money was coming from to repay his loan and no one need have worried a bit. Except the company's existing shareholders, of course.

Within a month the block of stock had been purchased, the old board of directors removed and five men very close to - and financially rewarded by - the mentor were the new policymakers at the company. Torrance himself couldn't be an officer or director – he wasn't yet eighteen years old – but he guided the movement of the company's cash from its bank account to those of Torrance and his mentor. Through management fees, expensive equipment leases from the mentor's company and other shenanigans, virtually all the cash was gone within a year.

The Financial Services Authority – the British equivalent to the U.S. Securities and Exchange Commission – took notice of the transactions only after small shareholders began to complain that the company was now worth far less than it had been before Torrance and his mentor took over. And they were right, but despite being unfortunate for them, it was perfectly legal. Thomas Newton Torrance and his mentor sold their stake at a small loss eighteen months after they had purchased it. Obviously the shares weren't worth as much as when Torrance had bought them – the company itself was worth less since it had been efficiently and effectively drained of about $16 million in cash. So the small loss in the share price didn't matter to Torrance and his boss – they had taken out a lot of money and were ready to move on.

Thomas Torrance repaid the £1 million loan his mentor had extended, leaving him with well over $6 million – not bad for an eighteen-year-old's first big deal. Over a celebratory dinner at Wilton's in London, Torrance announced his intention to try another acquisition, this time in the United States. He had been looking at public document filings and had come across another company that was remarkably similar to the one they'd just raided.

"What business is it in?" his mentor asked.

"They manufacture oil field equipment."

"No disrespect, Thomas, but what do you know about the oil field equipment business?"

That got a chuckle from Torrance. "Nothing, of course. But what does it matter? They have $8 million in cash. I know plenty about *that!*"

And he did. He formed a corporation and put the millions of pounds sterling from his last deal into it. Through that company he leased an apartment in New York – he was too young to sign legal documents on his own – then used more of his cash to purchase controlling interest in the oil field supply firm. Within twelve months Torrance had moved all the cash from this once-healthy company to his own coffers, leaving it with enough money to pay its bills but unable to grow its business in the future because of lack of capital.

The other shareholders ranted and screamed. The Wall Street Journal ran a story about Thomas Newton Torrance, applying the abbreviation "TNT" for the first time. "He's like dynamite to the companies he buys – the cash just implodes. Watch out for Thomas Newton Torrance – the TNT of the stock market!"

The article was less than flattering but with over $14 million in the bank, TNT was a success regardless. Although his activities raised regulatory eyebrows on both sides of the pond, everything he did was legal, even if it was unfair to the small shareholders and ethically reprehensible.

Three years passed and TNT was twenty-two. He had made six deals, successfully fended off four civil lawsuits by shareholders and two regulatory investigations (one each in London and New York) and he had accumulated a net worth of nearly $30 million.

Torrance discovered an interesting phenomenon that accompanied his success. Though he was certainly not handsome by any standard, he suddenly found it amazingly easy to attract beautiful women. They simply loved being with him. But then who wouldn't? TNT was in the society section of newspapers regularly – his corporation donated generously to political candidates, the arts and a dozen humanitarian causes. His motives were less than noble; the more he hobnobbed with the rich and famous, the easier it was to garner favors when the securities regulators came calling with a list of violations. The added bonus was the invitations that poured in almost weekly – a gallery opening here, a party at the Mayor's house there – and it wouldn't do to show up without a beautiful girl on your arm.

The society editors hadn't known exactly what to make of him. Everyone knew of his occasional run-ins with the regulators but he was likeable, outgoing and generous with the money he'd taken from the labors of others. TNT was like a firecracker to the society crowd in New York and London - shiny and sparkly but with a little touch of the dangerous thrown in.

There was one thing that was unusual about Thomas Newton Torrance. In every way that could be seen, he was a very religious man. He was an ordained minister in fact, thanks to a donation to an obscure school of religion in Mississippi. And TNT made sure his religious ways could be seen. As a successful entrepreneur Torrance counted as friends some of the highest leaders of the Protestant faith both in America and the United Kingdom. Once he became seriously wealthy he generously donated to causes connected with a variety of denominations. The common thread in his work for the Lord was that Thomas Newton Torrance cultivated friends in very high places, just as he did in his secular activities. When he attended a church service it wasn't a small congregation around the corner. It always was the most prominent church in New York or London or Los Angeles. He called ahead to make sure the senior pastor was aware he was coming and typically ended up with him at lunch or dinner after the service.

TNT carefully cultivated these connections. He inserted himself and his religiosity into the churches, lavishly spent money on projects suggested by the most influential people in the church and he curried favor from all. Sometimes when his business dealings were questioned he threw around names that helped legitimize him. If you can toss out the name of the nation's best-known television evangelist, or casually mention that the Archbishop of Canterbury was your guest for lunch last week, it sometimes made people question their own concerns. Maybe Thomas Newton Torrance wasn't an evil pillager of corporations after all. Maybe he was a real businessman – his connections with the church seemed to support that idea.

Now age forty, Thomas Newton Torrance was having a ball. Forbes Magazine ranked his worth near a billion dollars. His acquisitions grew larger and larger, his raids of corporate bank accounts more subtle and sophisticated but the results were always the same – TNT ended up with a lot of cash and the companies he briefly owned and controlled were the contributors of that bounty. With larger deals came more intense scrutiny and louder screams from his fellow shareholders who felt

THE STRANGEST THING

raped and pillaged after Torrance breezed through the bank accounts. Although he was forced to answer inquiries and subpoenas now and then, he continued to stay ahead of the game and had never been charged with a crime. The frequent publicity was negative but somehow never damaging enough to cause Torrance a major problem.

In 2012 Thomas Newton Torrance attended a party at the American Museum of Natural History on the Upper West Side in New York City. His date for the evening was a beautiful thirty-year-old who was a morning talk show host on NBC. The affair was a tribute to Sussex University's archaeology department and the contribution its teams of people had made. Over the past few decades it seemed people from Sussex were participating in practically every major dig in the world. The results had been very positive – the university and its professors were recognized regularly for their accomplishments and discoveries. It didn't hurt that the Indiana Jones and National Treasure movies had caused everyone to have a heightened interest in archaeology. Most digs were boring - they weren't looking for the Ark of the Covenant or the Holy Grail but more often finding out details about a civilization like the Inca or the Hittites. But the average guy on the street didn't know that. He thought Indy was fighting off tarantulas in the jungle to get the statue of solid gold. Archaeology had become exciting.

Archaeological programs take money and lots of it. Officials from Sussex threw the Natural History Museum party to educate wealthy potential donors about their programs and encourage them to invest. Senior professors from the archaeology and anthropology departments mingled with the guests, offering up interesting stories of hidden things in the jungles and under the desert sands of places far, far away. Thomas Torrance listened to one of those stories and became enthralled at what he heard.

At the end of the evening TNT looked up Dr. Martin Harvey, the vice president of the university and the senior person present at the event, and handed him a business card. "This is my mobile number," Torrance said. "Do you have time for a quick breakfast in the morning? I know you're busy – if you need to get back to the university early that's fine. I had a few questions and some thoughts for you."

Dr. Harvey had planned to catch the first train to Philadelphia, where he had left his car the previous morning. But the chance to meet with an interested party and potential donor whose net worth was in the hundreds of millions was too great an opportunity to pass up. He moved his Amtrak reservation to noon and at 7:30 a.m. was seated across from Thomas Torrance having breakfast at the Peninsula Hotel on Fifth Avenue. What he expected to be a quick meal turned into a lengthy question and answer session for both parties as they became acquainted. As the vice president listened he began to understand the particular interest Thomas Newton Torrance had and the one very specific, highly unusual project he wanted to fund.

THE STRANGEST THING

The vice president of Sussex University could hardly contain his excitement on the trip home. He had received a commitment from Torrance for $10 million to fund a project in Palenque, Mexico that had languished for years. This particular dig had proven more difficult than most for attracting donors - it had a very unusual purpose.

In 1952 the tomb of King Pakal was discovered far beneath the Temple of the Inscriptions at Palenque. This discovery rekindled ancient stories - tales of strange things hidden even deeper in the ground. Present day Mayans recalled accounts passed down by the ancients. Speaking in whispers and only among themselves – never with the Spanish conquerors or other white men – the elders kept alive a fascinating tale of an ancient chamber discovered during Pakal's reign. The room was said to be far, far older than the Mayan civilization and to contain a puzzling object. The king's advisors couldn't explain the artifact and considered it sacred. According to the legend, Pakal ordered it left alone where it lay on a stone altar. Then he ordered his own tomb to be built atop the ancient chamber. Finally, Pakal constructed the massive Temple of the Inscriptions above his tomb – an edifice that today rose above the trees in the jungle and was considered one of the most beautiful ancient Mayan structures.

Sussex archaeologists had wanted to send a team to Palenque to explore the chamber housing Pakal's sarcophagus. Was there a far older secret than the Maya themselves? No one knew *what* was supposed to be there – only that the rumors had persisted for hundreds of years and that many Mayans even today believed *something* was there – something unbelievably ancient.

It would be a difficult project because of the historic significance of Pakal's tomb and sarcophagus. Obtaining a permit to move the King's body or his coffin would be impossible. Even with the prestigious Sussex University leading the project it was unlikely the Mexican authorities would be convinced of the value of any intrusion into this important site. So the dig went unfunded for several years, relegated to the back burner while the university continued its work at major sites around the globe.

Now however the university vice president had a funding commitment. The breakfast with the man they called TNT had been an interesting one. Dr. Harvey had handed Torrance a substantial packet of information about Sussex and its extensive archaeological department and programs, but TNT hadn't even given it a glance. In fact, the vice president noted, Torrance left it sitting on the table when they departed the hotel. From the very beginning of the conversation TNT had wanted to know only about the Palenque project, the one that had sat for years with no permits and no funding. This was the sole endeavor he was interested in.

As the train sped west through Pennsylvania Dr. Harvey made notes. There was a lot of work ahead before this project could begin. Torrance had insisted it start with the summer digging season – only a few months away. But the academician had cautioned him that the permit process would be long and difficult. His expectations for a summer dig were unrealistic.

Thomas Newton Torrance's response had surprised Dr. Harvey. He had laughed. "I've found that greasing the wheels makes the machine move faster. I'd be pleased to be involved in the initial discussions Sussex has with the archaeological authorities in Mexico City. I'm certain I can be of assistance in getting things moving."

From experience Dr. Harvey felt TNT was overly optimistic. *He's like most of the wealthy patrons I've seen,* the man thought to himself. *He thinks throwing money at a problem will solve it. I don't think that's going to work this time.*

But he was certainly willing to give it a try. Ten million dollars didn't come along every day and this project would give the university major publicity if it came to fruition. And if there really *were* secrets under the temple . . . well, that could be exponentially more valuable for Sussex.

As things turned out Thomas Newton Torrance was both right and wrong. Things happened, but not because of his ability to grease wheels in the Mexican government. In fact Torrance had no involvement at all in getting the permits Sussex needed. The wheels were greased all right, but in an entirely different way and by a totally different person than TNT – a man with even more power and influence than the outgoing, slightly shady near-billionaire Englishman.

When Dr. Martin Harvey arrived back on the campus of Sussex University he went straight to the office of the college president and broke the news of a $10 million commitment to begin the long-delayed exploration at Palenque. He told his boss he thought the permit process would be a lengthy and difficult one – impossible, perhaps.

"The body of King Pakal still lies in its sarcophagus eighty feet down inside the temple," he said. "I can't imagine the Mexican archaeological authorities allowing us to dig right next to it, but we would have to because the room is so small. I'm excited about Mr. Torrance's commitment to the project but I have to confess I doubt we will see it happen for years, if at all."

The university president seemed both thrilled at the news and unconcerned at Dr. Harvey's pessimism about how long things might take.

"I have a secret weapon. I don't know if it'll work or not but I think Sussex has a better chance to make this happen than any other institution."

Dr. Martin Harvey didn't know what his boss meant by that. But he soon found out as things began to happen incredibly quickly.

The first call the university president made was to his old Sussex fraternity brother and current United States Ambassador to Mexico. After the Ambassador heard the news, the two old friends talked about John Chapman, the President of the United States. Archaeology was

Chapman's passion. Since he took office the President had spent hundreds of thousands of dollars of his own money funding projects he found interesting. Both men thought the President would love this one. It had mystery and adventure written all over it.

The Ambassador made just one call, President Chapman just one more, and the deal was done. It was just that simple. Sussex University got its permits. A team would be digging at the Temple of the Inscriptions in the summer to see if there was anything to the Mayan legend of an ancient artifact hidden deep within the earth.

Dr. Harvey had called Thomas Newton Torrance the moment the permits were approved. After offering congratulations TNT said, "I'd like to request that one of your graduate students be the supervisor of the dig at Palenque. Although I don't know him personally I've followed the work of Cory Spencer. I'd consider it a personal favor if he oversaw the project, reporting of course to the university but keeping me informed as well."

And as easily as that the wealthy entrepreneur got the man he wanted installed as supervisor. Cory Spencer would lead the search for an artifact TNT believed would shake the world's foundations.

CHAPTER FIVE

A national security briefing document was slipped under the President's bedroom door early every morning along with the Washington Post. When he awoke, Chapman retrieved them both and returned to bed, where he liked to watch TV and have his first cup of coffee. Chapman had one additional document delivered each day – privately he considered this one far more interesting than the top-secret daily briefing. The night staff used Google to search for keywords and generated a paper, sometimes only a couple of pages long but sometimes more than twenty and often filled with pictures. This document kept President Chapman on top of things happening in the adventure and intrigue of archaeological excavations around the world.

In one recent document President Chapman had seen Thomas Newton Torrance's name. He had heard of Torrance before – the financier's escapades made the financial press regularly – but his dealings weren't significant or interesting enough to capture the President's attention. This time Chapman saw Torrance's name in an article about the new dig at Palenque. The archaeological publication chose to paint a very flattering picture of the entrepreneur, ignoring the activities that others termed corporate raiding or outright banditry. It called Torrance an entrepreneur and a generous man, eager to fund his passionate interest in archaeology – an interesting comment given that no one had ever linked TNT with the field prior to this one large donation. For a fleeting moment as he read the article, the President wondered what the real motive was for this British entrepreneur's decision to spend a huge sum on what could be a complete wild goose chase.

The President breezed through today's two briefing papers as the Gulfstream flew toward the Gulf of Mexico on the twenty-five hundred mile, four hour trip. Chapman had brought along an old dog-eared guidebook to the Mayan ruins at Palenque. It had accompanied his first two trips to the site years ago and he wanted to refresh himself about the Temple of the Inscriptions before seeing it again this morning.

In his call two days ago the Ambassador to Mexico had told President Chapman some details of the discovery. The permit to excavate which the Mexican government had issued to Sussex University's team had contained very strong restrictions. These were designed to ensure there would be no danger to the tomb of King Pakal, especially to the sarcophagus and its lid, which contained priceless carvings including some of the most detailed and exquisite Mayan glyphs ever discovered.

Deep inside the Temple of the Inscriptions the university's dig supervisor, Cory Spencer, and a team of students had worked while a motor droned far above, pumping fresh air into the claustrophobic chamber. The room was hot and stuffy and so crowded that only two or three team members could work at a time. They were not allowed to place any of their equipment on the sarcophagus itself. That meant even less room to work was available between the stone coffin and the walls of its crypt - only a few feet on each side of the sarcophagus.

A representative of the National Institute of Archaeology and History was assigned to monitor the dig site while excavations were underway. The team tried non-invasive ways to discover openings or rooms around or below the tomb chamber including sonar that couldn't penetrate the massive stones. Spencer, the team leader, secured the representative's approval for a minimally invasive plan. The diggers ran long narrow steel rods through the seams between the rocks in the floor and walls of Pakal's tomb chamber. If a cavity were behind the rocks they hoped the rods would slide through the dirt, allowing the crew to snake a camera inside to see what was there.

The diggers performed this exercise almost fifty times, inching their way along the walls and floor, and found nothing but solid dirt. After hours one of the female students was still trying, pushing the rod slowly through a crack between two floor stones. She felt the rod move through unyielding dirt but suddenly become easy to push. She had reached open space under the stone!

She scampered up the ancient stairway seventy-five feet to the top of the temple and told the dig's leader what she had found. Cory grabbed a flexible hose with a camera mounted to its tip and went back down into the tomb with her. They bent down to the floor and inserted the hose through the hole where the steel rod had penetrated. The rock was about two feet in height so it took only a moment for the camera hose to clear the rock and hang freely in midair. Cory turned on the camera and looked at a handheld TV screen to which the hose was connected. It was difficult to discern what the camera showed because the area below was dim and the light from the tiny camera faint.

He was encouraged. "This indicates there's likely a room beneath this floor. The camera's so small that it can't see very far and I detect nothing solid like walls – hopefully that means there's a considerable open space below us."

The team went to their bunks that night excited at the possibilities. Spencer and the governmental archaeology representative on site discussed plans and the latter made a call to Mexico City. He spoke with Dr. Armando Ortiz, the director – *el jefe* - of the National Institute of Archaeology and History. He was the person in charge of all archaeological digs in the country – the nation's lead archaeologist. Ortiz personally arrived at Palenque the next afternoon, a clear sign of how significant he considered this news.

It took a week for the university team and the archaeology representatives to reach an agreement. It was decided that the diggers would remove a two-foot square stone – the one the girl had worked on when she found the hole. They would feed hooks on lines down all four sides of the stone then winch it up, all without touching the sarcophagus of King Pakal only inches away. The slightest error could damage one of the most important relics of the Maya period – the lid of Pakal's tomb.

After they removed that single stone a larger light could be lowered into the cavity to see how much area they were working with and what the room, if that's what it was, contained. With that information they could decide what to do next.

The team fashioned a pulley system that would be hung from a platform over the stone they were removing. The platform would stand above and to the right of Pakal's sarcophagus on wooden legs and it would be braced with struts to keep it away from the stone coffin and lid. They submitted their plans to the governmental representative who sent them on to Dr. Ortiz in Mexico City. Approval came surprisingly quickly and nearly three weeks after the discovery they were at last ready to lift the stone.

On the appointed day three people stood in the cramped space around Pakal's crypt – Ortiz, Cory Spencer and the girl who had found the space. Three others were on the stone stairway, their hands on the apparatus that would allow the pulley to raise the rock from the floor. The sarcophagus, next to which the pulley system had been constructed, was wrapped in blankets and foam more than a foot thick to protect the ornate lid from any accidents.

Given the signal from the leader the men began to turn a wheel and tighten the wires that ran from the pulley down below the rock on four sides. The wooden structure groaned and creaked as the wires grew more and more taut. Everyone could hear the strain being put on the wires as they tightened around several hundred pounds of rock. Cory Spencer cast a worried glance at the archaeology representative. If this whole thing collapsed it could be disaster for the sarcophagus lid.

Everyone in the room held a collective breath as the rock moved upwards about a half inch. "Easy, easy," Cory said in a whisper as he watched the progress.

The men who operated the winch moved the rock very, very slowly. It took nearly two hours before it was completely out of its resting place. As Cory and the girl carefully moved the rock to the right the winch operators lowered it to the floor. Now there was a twenty-four inch hole in the ground with only blackness inside the opening. Spencer picked up a powerful light, switched it on and directed it into the chamber they had unearthed. The others heard him gasp. "Oh my God," he whispered. "Oh my God."

Dr. Ortiz stood next to Cory Spencer. He leaned forward and caught a glimpse just as Spencer shut off the light and stood up.

43

"What is it?" he asked Cory.

"You know what's next, sir. Let's go to the top. I have to make a call."

Immediately the others spoke up. The girl who found the hole said, "Can't we show the rest of the team what's down there? It's only fair . . ."

Talking over her, Dr. Ortiz yelled, "I want to see it!"

Spencer responded with an attitude they hadn't heard from him before. It was abrupt, harsh, and curt. His face was serious. He looked at Ortiz. "You know about this. You know what has to happen next. I don't think you want to override my instructions."

To the others he said, "Get out of the tomb, all of you. Now. I report to people just like you do. I have to make a call."

The student diggers were amazed to see Dr. Ortiz, the highest archaeological authority in the country, acquiesce to Cory Spencer. They all climbed the stairs and emerged on top of the Temple of the Inscriptions, just as Spencer had ordered them to do.

Cory called the U.S. Ambassador and told him what had been found. The diplomat assumed his was the first call Cory made after the discovery. But it was actually Cory's *second* call.

THE STRANGEST THING

After Spencer had ushered everyone out of the temple the team from Sussex University didn't know what to think. In the plaza outside they talked among themselves about their leader's possible motive in shutting them out of the discovery one of them had made. Within an hour after the men had opened the hole, Cory had ordered his team completely off the site with instructions not to return until further notice. Likewise, Dr. Ortiz commanded the Temple of the Inscriptions closed to the public. He then drove back to Mexico City.

That left no one at the site for two days except Cory Spencer and the person to whom he had first called to report the discovery. During that time Spencer showed the man what had been found. Strings had been pulled in Mexico City that allowed these two people unrestricted access with no governmental oversight.

Thomas Newton Torrance was accustomed to pulling strings. In fact he was a master at it.

CHAPTER SIX
Thursday
The day of the disappearance

President Chapman's excitement mounted as the SUV arrived at the ancient site of Palenque. The driver pulled into a gravel lot. As usual the Secret Service agents exited the vehicle, scanned the area then allowed the President out.

Dr. Ortiz had learned about the upcoming visit in a call from the President of Mexico the previous morning. He drove back to Palenque to welcome the party. A heavy man, he was dressed in a wrinkled suit that had seen better days. His open collar shirt was stained with sweat and he sported a scuffed pith helmet. The heat of the jungle was oppressive but Ortiz had worn his finest clothes. It wasn't every day that an American President made a secret trip to Mexico, and then to a ruin under the supervision of Dr. Ortiz! He wasn't going to miss an opportunity to show off the famous site and perhaps even get his picture taken with el Presidente Chapman.

Ortiz introduced the President to Thomas Newton Torrance, explaining that Torrance was the British financier who had funded the project at Palenque. TNT was dressed impeccably in a white linen suit. He looked like the star from the old TV show *Fantasy Island*. The President thought he seemed totally out of place here in the jungle.

"It's a pleasure to have you at the site, Mr. President."

"Thanks, Mr. Torrance. I recently read of your involvement here but I didn't know you had an interest in the Maya."

Chapman and Torrance chatted as Ortiz led them down a wooded path that opened into a broad courtyard. There were several ancient structures around a much larger one. "The Palace," Ortiz announced to the group as he gestured proudly toward the massive building. "And here, next to it, The Temple of the Inscriptions."

Sunlight broke through the high trees surrounding the courtyard and illuminated the top of the Temple. The President looked up and saw a view he'd marveled at before – on top of the temple nearly eighty feet above the jungle floor sat a small building with five dark open doorways. It was through one of those doors that the

President would find the stairway leading down deep inside the building, to the tomb of King Pakal.

Chapman's excitement grew as the men climbed seven stories, their knees straining as they navigated the very tall rock stairs the Mayans typically used in their architecture. No one knew why the builders created steps too tall to scale in a normal gait. Since it was only priests and royalty who ascended to the top, some scholars figured the difficult stairway was a sign from the priests that the common people shouldn't attempt to navigate their ways to the top. Maybe the holy men were sending a message that the road was too tough for anyone but the anointed. But no one knew for sure.

At the top they entered the doorway leading to Pakal's tomb. A hole in the floor of that room was the place where Alberto Ruz had discovered the hidden staircase in 1952. Now it was open and ready for descent but by only one person at a time.

"Are the lights on all the way down?" the President asked Dr. Ortiz.

"Yes, el Presidente. I will lead the way for you."

Chapman turned to Ortiz. "I've been here before. I'll do it alone. I want to experience what you've found by myself."

"Ah, of course." The director's disappointment shone clearly on his face. "No hay problema, el Presidente. Here is my strong torch for you to take through the opening into the new chamber. The Sussex University crew has removed the rock in the floor. The hole is still tight but you will fit fine. I put a ladder down into the room below for you. Other than the archaeological team and me, you will be the first to see the thing the diggers discovered."

One of the Secret Service agents tapped the President's arm lightly. "May I have a word with you, sir?"

"No, you may not," the President said curtly. "I want to see this, to stand alone and take in whatever they've found. I've heard enough to know it's astounding at least. I'll be fine. I know with all this rock you won't be able to communicate with me. But I'm only seventy-five feet away – straight down this stairway. There's only one way in and one way out. Give me fifteen minutes. If I'm not standing right back up here with you by then, come find me. I may have been overcome with the wonder of whatever it is!" He laughed and started down the stone staircase. At the halfway point it took a turn and the party above lost sight of him.

As they awaited John Chapman's return, Torrance asked Dr. Ortiz where Cory Spencer was. "Since he's the chief man on the dig, I thought he would be here in case the President had questions. Did you send him off somewhere?"

"No," Ortiz responded. "I haven't seen him at all this morning. It's unusual, actually. He's always here early."

Torrance thought about that, pulled out his phone and sent a text to Cory Spencer. He heard nothing – that was rare since Spencer was under strict orders to answer him immediately.

The President's self-imposed quarter-hour deadline passed. He didn't return.

Fifteen minutes on the dot after the President had left, an alarm buzzed on the Secret Service agent's watch. "Let's go," he said to his partner.

"We'll all go," Dr. Ortiz said nervously, louder than he intended. Things were not going well on his watch, at his temple.

The agent responded firmly. "No. No time to talk. The two of us go. You'll stay here." They started quickly down the stairs. As they descended Torrance and Ortiz watched them unstrap the safety buckles that secured the revolver each carried on his belt.

Within a couple of minutes they were in Pakal's tomb. The sarcophagus lid was still covered in protective layers and to one side sat a large stone. The top of a ladder stuck out of a hole in the floor where the rock had been. One of the agents retrieved a flashlight, shone it into the area below and yelled, "Mr. President. Are you there?"

There was no response. The agents scrambled down the ladder into a room with solid rock walls, very similar to Pakal's tomb chamber just above it. The room was a ten-foot cube. There was some type of rock altar in the middle. Lying on it was what appeared to be a crumpled piece of metal about eight feet long and three feet wide. It was clearly something manufactured. The object was roughly a long triangle with holes in it that might have served to increase its tensile strength. One of the agents thought it looked like a very large version of the fins that form the base of rockets people shoot on the Fourth of July.

The agents gave the object a brief glance. Their eyes swept the room searching for President Chapman. He was not there. They did a quick check of the walls and floor to see if anything appeared out of place. There had to be another way out of this chamber but the men couldn't see it. Every rock, every seam in walls, floor and ceiling looked as though they had been untouched for hundreds of years.

Back at the top one of the agents asked Dr. Ortiz if there was any other entrance or exit from the stairway, Pakal's tomb chamber or the newly discovered room below it. Ortiz responded that since the discovery the diggers had searched every square inch. They were convinced there was no other way in or out.

The other agent was on his cellphone, his hands shaking as he said words he had never hoped to utter. "Eagle is missing. Repeat, Eagle is missing."

CHAPTER SEVEN
Sunday
Three days after the disappearance

President John Chapman disappeared on a Thursday. By Sunday the entire country anxiously waited for the other shoe to drop. Someone had to know where he was – someone had taken him. Unless, that is, he had fallen through a secret hole into a deep well. Or been abducted by aliens. Or decided to disappear for reasons known only to him.

Theories ranged from reasonable to wacky and the authorities attempted to deal with them logically. Both the FBI and the Secret Service struggled to be productive. On the day the President disappeared the Secret Service agents worked for hours in tandem with the Mexican Federal Police, combing every square inch of Pakal's tomb and the newly discovered chamber below it.

THE STRANGEST THING

They stopped their efforts at dusk after finding absolutely nothing. At the top of the staircase Dr. Ortiz, the national archaeological director, closed and locked the heavy iron gate that covered the stairs. He posted a guard in the plaza at the base of the temple and the FBI assigned two men there as well. The search for President Chapman would resume in the morning.

In his role as director of the National Institute, Dr. Ortiz walked a fine line between sympathy for the situation and the need to ensure the preservation of King Pakal's sarcophagus. Try as everyone might to find an answer, there were no leads and no clues by Sunday.

First Lady Marianne Chapman's grief was tangible. Gut-wrenching sobs wracked her body. The rare times she left the personal residence during those first few days people saw a woman whose eyes were bloodshot and puffy from tears. Her staff felt genuinely sorry for her and pondered what it must be like to have your husband just disappear.

The First Lady's torment and tears were real. She grieved inconsolably. Not for her husband, of course. Her love for him had been gone so long she hardly remembered if it ever actually had existed. She cried because there were no children to stand beside her. Thanks to her husband and his selfish desires to further his career, he had emphatically insisted there was no time or place for children. As a young bride she accepted it, certain his mind would change later. But that one statement by an aspiring young politician turned out to be the first of many which turned his new wife against him, creating a decades-long loveless marriage.

No, Marianne Chapman's tears were for herself. She knew if her husband didn't come back all the things she loved would end abruptly. She would be packed up and shipped out of the White House the instant Harry Harrison was inaugurated President.

She loved the attention she got as the President's wife. She craved it, thrived on it. The First Lady had thrown away her own life to be the wife of a powerful man. She had lost the chance for a family, the love of a husband and a truly meaningful life. And now, thanks to the son of a bitch who had gotten lost somewhere, she stood to lose the only thing she cared about any more – the love and attention of millions of people, the cover pictures on magazines, the fawning, pawing pushes as people tried to shake her hand in a crowd. No matter that it wasn't real. No matter than people didn't *really* love her – in fact they didn't even *know* her. She was about to lose it all. She was about to be a has-been – a *former* First Lady.

Marianne Chapman had been the first person in the USA questioned by the FBI. Asked by an agent if her husband had appeared worried or atypically concerned the morning he flew to Palenque, she responded, "I don't know. I didn't see him that morning. He, uh, he left really early and I had decided to sleep in another bedroom that night so he wouldn't wake me." All that was true - she *never* slept with her husband.

THE STRANGEST THING

Every news broadcast led with the story of the American leader's disappearance. The daily banner on CNN read "The Missing President." The countdown of days since Chapman disappeared had started on day two, Saturday. But soon the reports became briefer and briefer – there was no update, nothing new to report and camera footage was always the same – shots from outside the Temple of the Inscriptions showing a plethora of police and governmental vehicles from both the USA and Mexico parked randomly in the grassy areas between the ancient buildings. News teams could film at the base of the temple but were not allowed to climb the structure. Trucks with satellite dishes sat in the main parking lot of the temple complex, cables running down the same path the President had walked only days before.

The first news helicopters had arrived on Friday, hoping to hover a hundred feet off the ground and shoot footage inside the building atop the temple, where the stairway led down to the tomb that John Chapman had entered. As the first blades whirred noisily at the top of the Temple of the Inscriptions, blowing dirt and trees around down below, the Archaeological Director screamed at the chopper from the ground, shaking his fist. "Get away! Get away! You'll harm the structure!"

Within twenty minutes Dr. Ortiz had a governmental order closing the airspace over the Mayan city of Palenque. The news crews were grounded. Literally.

Back in Washington, something had to be done about succession. There was no precedent for this situation. Within twenty-four hours of Chapman's disappearance the Vice President had been briefed on all the critical situations in the nation and the world. But without the authority to act Harry Harrison was powerless. He couldn't order policy changes, send troops into battle or move to stabilize the economy. He had only the specific powers of his own office, not those of the missing Commander-in-Chief.

Most of Washington considered it a foregone conclusion that the Vice President would be sworn in to succeed John Chapman. The country had to have a leader and it had to be done quickly. But the events of the past week were unprecedented in America's nearly two hundred and fifty years of existence. Never before had there been the question of removing a President from office simply because he was missing. No one knew exactly how things could be done to make succession a reality. In a rare moment of unity, the leaders of both houses turned to the Supreme Court.

Everyone close to the situation walked on eggshells – no one wanted his or her thoughts or words to upset First Lady Marianne Chapman, underplay the life of her husband or make it appear as though the Vice President were eager to assume the Presidency. After all, no one knew if President Chapman was still alive. Despite the largest and most intensive manhunt in history, not a single clue had emerged as to the President's whereabouts. No one had heard a word. No demands. No video of a bound and gagged prisoner. No ransom letter. Nothing at all.

Marianne Chapman made a phone call to the only Justice her husband had named to the Supreme Court. She pleaded with him through sobs of anguish to hold off on naming the Vice President as her husband's successor. "They'll find John, I'm sure. He's just lost. Don't let the Court do this." To the Justice Mrs. Chapman sounded like the grief-stricken wife he would have expected her to be, tormented by the disappearance of her husband and distraught at the lack of any news whatsoever. He promised the First Lady he would consider her request. He quietly reminded her, however, that the Court had to do what was best for the country as a whole.

The First Lady hung up knowing she had little time left in the life she loved, the one to which she had become so accustomed. From her bedroom that afternoon her screams of grief could be heard all over the residence on the second floor of the White House. The staff went about their duties in silence, heads hung low, each of them incorrectly believing her anguish was over the disappearance of her husband.

CHAPTER EIGHT
Thursday
Seven days after the disappearance

The day of the Supreme Court's decision on succession was a frenzied one in the White House. Now at least everyone knew what would come next. Now everyone had direction for the future of the nation.

The Oval Office had been eerily quiet for seven days. No one sat in the President's chair. No meetings were held in this historic chamber. Doors were kept closed and the room was dark – the office was unoccupied, awaiting the high court's ruling on whether John Chapman would officially be a past President or remain the Commander-in-Chief in absentia.

During the past week Vice President Harry Harrison had conducted a dozen meetings with his Chief of Staff, Bob Parker, and other key members of his team as everyone waited for the Supreme Court to hand down a decision. What would in normal circumstances be called the VP's transition team was instead vaguely termed his "summit group." They had had a couple of meetings with President Chapman's top people but once again everyone refrained from too much assumption. Tempers were short on the Chapman side – none of his staff was willing to turn over the reins when the President's whereabouts remained unknown. They wanted to keep their jobs. For the Vice President, understatement was paramount. No one wanted to appear presumptuous or anticipatory – most of all the Vice President himself. He had to patiently wait for guidance.

At nine a.m. on the seventh day after President John Chapman went missing the Chief Justice of the Supreme Court phoned Vice President Harrison. It was a courtesy call with advance notice about the decision that would be made public a half hour later. As soon as the call ended, Harry Harrison walked over to his office door, opened it and yelled across the room to his Chief of Staff, "Bob! Get the team in here now!" Glancing at his appointments secretary, he said, "Cancel everything for today," then strode back to his desk.

When his team was assembled, Harry Harrison told them about the call he had received. "I'm going to be sworn in as President this afternoon at three p.m.," he said. "It'll be low key. The Chief Justice asked me where I wanted the ceremony and I chose the Oval Office.

Now folks, let's spend the next hour going over everyone's tasks and responsibilities going forward."

One after another his people reported on task lists that had been theoretical but were now ready to implement. The Chief of Staff had assigned projects to ten staffers who made up the team. They had run two scenarios – one with Harry Harrison remaining Vice President but being appointed "interim President" with expanded powers in the President's absence. The other was in preparation for exactly what was going to happen – their boss becoming the next President.

"What happens if Chapman shows back up in a week or two?" one staffer asked.

"The Chief Justice told me they had unanimously agreed this had to be a permanent transition of power. It's too complicated otherwise. It could potentially create a major problem with allies and enemies alike. We can't be seen as weak and leaderless. He said for the good of the country and the American people I would assume the presidency for the remainder of President Chapman's term. That's what I agreed to do."

As much as anyone could be a friend of the irascible John Chapman, he and Vice President Harrison had been amiable colleagues before the campaign and remained so afterwards. They had served together in the Senate and worked closely on major legislation. Chapman had involved his second-in-command in strategic decisions much more than previous Presidents had done. Harrison had even had input into the selection of the President's cabinet. All that would be helpful as Harry Harrison assumed the highest office in the nation.

The team's immediate focus was on the swearing-in ceremony to be held in less than six hours. They sought the Vice President's guidance on who would attend and whether there would be any sort of gathering of friends and family afterwards. Harrison's first address to the nation was also critical. It had to happen immediately after he assumed the presidency - one staffer left the meeting after getting feedback on what Harry Harrison wanted. He had work to do, quickly. He was the man who would draft the new President's acceptance speech.

At three p.m. on the seventh day after the disappearance of John Chapman, he was officially removed from office and replaced by President William Henry Harrison IV of Oklahoma. The Chief Justice administered the oath of office before a small group of people including former First Lady Marianne Chapman, Harrison's wife and two children, the leaders of both houses of Congress, the Chairman of the Joint Chiefs of Staff and all members of the Cabinet. It was a somber occasion – there was no jovial backslapping. The congratulatory handshakes were muted and subdued. It was not a happy time. It was a time when the American people didn't know if they should mourn or be hopeful. Was the President dead? No one knew, but life had to go on. Especially at the summit of the greatest and most powerful nation on earth.

Harry Harrison sat in the Oval Office at five p.m., having just finished his first speech as President of the United States. It had gone well – mostly it was an assurance to the people that things would continue as they had been - the programs of the government, its commitments to allies and negotiations with those who stood against it – these would proceed without major change. The new President had expressed regret that his Presidency came as part of such a horrifying event and had offered a prayer for John Chapman and his wife.

The entire oration was crafted in an attempt to calm the nation. There was a growing faction of people who was incensed that President Chapman was being "dethroned" through no fault of his own. Many people were outraged at the President's removal from office despite the country's need for a leader and the uncertainty of Chapman's situation. Some of those people had demonstrated their anger in dangerous ways. In the past few days there had been bomb threats, men with handguns arrested near the White House fence, intelligence chatter from terrorist groups who believed it was time to strike the wicked and leaderless America while it was floundering.

From the minute Chapman disappeared security in the nation's capital had been increased dramatically. Everyone was on heightened alert and the President expected things would continue this way until there was an answer about John Chapman's disappearance. He just hoped that answer would come soon.

THE STRANGEST THING

The hardest thing for the FBI to imagine was that someone had planned the leader's kidnapping with no desire to extract anything from America because of it. But the total lack of communication was puzzling. The new President and the FBI director discussed "what-if's" – what if Chapman had been locked away in a hidden location, perhaps even buried in a box underground, then the kidnapper had somehow died? What if no one alive knew the President's whereabouts? Why had no one heard a word? Could it be possible this wasn't a kidnapping at all, but the President had instead fallen somewhere inside a passage in the ruin and become trapped? The country could go years – perhaps forever – without an answer if one of these things had happened.

The frustration of the United States Ambassador to Mexico was growing by the hour. The staff of the Embassy in Mexico City had been issued specific orders by the Ambassador himself. They were instructed to obtain permission to probe the depths of the temple. John Chapman had gone in and never come out. There was something else there and the United States was going to use every means in its power to find out what.

So far nothing had worked. While sympathetic to the situation, the Mexican authorities refused to be pushed into allowing the FBI or American archaeologists to invasively explore the ancient rooms below the Temple of the Inscriptions. Two calls from the Vice President had done nothing to change the mind of the Mexican government.

Now that he was inaugurated Harrison had the full power of the highest office in the nation. He spoke with the U.S. Ambassador then called the President of Mexico. In the harshest words imaginable Harrison stated his case. It had been seven days since President Chapman disappeared from one of two chambers, both of which appeared impregnable. The FBI had been allowed to scour the walls, ceilings and floors and to use non-invasive devices to attempt to see what lay behind the stones, but the Mexican government would not grant permission to destroy walls or floors in order to ascertain where the President might have gone.

Harry Harrison listened as the President of Mexico responded. The government's position had not changed, the President said. The tomb and the chamber with the artifact were too archaeologically significant, ancient and fragile to allow tampering, even for something as important as this.

"Realistically, President Harrison," the leader of Mexico said, "there is no way President Chapman is still inside the tomb. It just defies logic. Somehow he made his way out or was taken away. I assure you that our officials are presently looking into every possibility and checking all means of entering or leaving the structure. But for now that is all I can give you. We will keep trying but we will not allow alteration or destruction of our monument for any reason. Period."

And there was nothing the United States could do about it.

CHAPTER NINE
Friday
Eight days after the disappearance

Brian Sadler walked the twenty or so blocks from his Upper West Side apartment to Bijan Rarities, the antiquities gallery he owned on Fifth Avenue. This morning the weather was unseasonably cool for early June but the forecast was for a warm afternoon. Brian enjoyed cutting through Central Park; you avoided a lot of pedestrians on the sidewalks and he found the park peaceful and beautiful as the trees sported new leaves for summer.

He exited the park and walked four blocks south on Fifth Avenue. The buzz and excitement of Manhattan still got to him even though he'd been a resident for several years. He would always be a Texan at heart – they say you can't take the country out of a boy – but he had adapted very well to life in the Big Apple. He felt fortunate that he had the resources to enjoy everything the city had to offer.

It was almost 8:30 a.m. when Brian unlocked the front door and disarmed the gallery's elaborate security system. He walked to a massive vault door and entered a series of numbers that would begin the sequence of disarming the time delay lock.

Brian's second-in-command, Collette Conning, would be coming in around 9:45 – unless he had an early meeting Brian always timed his arrival an hour or so ahead of her. It was his quiet time to read a couple of papers and catch up on email. Most people in their thirties had long since stopped reading the newspaper in hard copy – everyone seemed to get his news online these days – but there was something comforting to Brian about sitting at his desk, reading page after page of the Times and the Wall Street Journal, marking things he would later ask Collette to clip, file or research for him.

Bijan Rarities had expanded dramatically since the days when the gallery's founder Darius Nazir and Brian had teamed up. Nazir's untimely death and a generous bequest had given Brian the chance to strike out on his own, leaving the highflying world of stocks and becoming a major player in the rarities markets around the globe. Brian had obtained the Bethlehem Scroll, one of the most significant objects ever discovered. He had engaged his passion for archaeology by visiting remote sites in the Middle East and South America. He and his girlfriend Nicole Farber had gone to Belize and Guatemala to find

THE STRANGEST THING

Mayan artifacts in an ancient city high in the clouds. Things had gotten out of hand quickly – Brian was trapped hundreds of feet below the surface in a Mayan cave and his and Nicole's subsequent kidnappings could have cost them their lives.

Adventure intrigued Brian. His harrowing experiences only made him yearn for more. Dallas and New York, the cities Nicole and Brian respectively called home, were exciting and fun for him but he frequently found himself thinking how he could get to the places he considered really exciting. Back to the jungle – back to ancient things and the thrill of being on yet another search for antiquities.

He fixed a cup of coffee and sat at his desk. The headlines of both papers spoke of Vice President Harry Harrison's ascension to the Presidency. Brian read the stories closely because of his personal interest in Harrison. The pictures showed a somber group of attendees, a stoic Harrison raising his right hand as he recited the oath of office and excerpts from the speech he had given to the nation afterwards. Brian had listened to every word of that speech; since it had been given during a busy workday for Brian, he had recorded and watched it in bed last night.

For yet another day, there was no news about the whereabouts of former President John Chapman. It was as though he had dropped off the face of the earth. Several times Brian had been to Palenque and the Temple of the Inscriptions, the place from which Chapman disappeared. Brian had read the stories telling about the strange chamber found below the tomb of King Pakal and the artifact that had been discovered there fascinated him.

But where was President Chapman? He had gone into the temple, descended into its bowels and never returned. The news reporters said the FBI had tried searches with ground-penetrating radar to determine if more chambers existed beside or beneath the one recently discovered. The technology had proven useless because of the building's solid rock walls.

There had to be another way out. The President hadn't just vaporized into thin air, so if he went in but didn't come back up the same stairway, he had to have gone somewhere else. But there *was* no place else. So far, eight days after his disappearance, no one had discovered what or where that place was.

Hearing five beeps, Brian walked to the vault door, entered a code and unlocked it. He swung it open, revealing a jail-like wall of bars with a gate. Inside the vault were shelves and pedestals with Bijan's most precious pieces. When Collette arrived, some of these would be moved to the showroom floor for display to the public.

Brian's office phone quietly rang. He went to his desk and saw a blinking light indicating it was his private line, a number that very few people had. He glanced at his watch – it was just after nine – and picked up the phone.

THE STRANGEST THING

"Good morning, Mr. Sadler," a pleasant female voice said. "This is the White House with a call from President Harrison. May I put the call through, sir?"

Brian smiled. "Of course," he said. She put him on hold.

After less than a minute he heard, "Well hello, Brian. I guess you've heard about my promotion."

"Mr. President, I want to offer congratulations, even though I know it's a tough way for you to become the Chief Executive."

"Absolutely. And Brian, when it's just us we can drop the 'Mr. President' stuff? I appreciate your respect for the office but you and I go too far back. And we'll never hurt each other, will we?"

That made Brian laugh. Since they were roommates at the University of Oklahoma they had joked that each of them had "the pictures" and neither of them could afford to hurt the other. The "pictures" didn't exist but there were a lot of crazy, stupid escapades the two college friends had done together that the general public didn't need to know about. And wouldn't.

"No, Harry. We'll never hurt each other. But I know you're a busy man – in fact I guess yesterday afternoon you became the busiest man in the world. What do you need from your old roommate? I don't think there's much I have that you could use at this point."

"You're wrong about that, Brian. The night I became Vice President you asked me not to forget you. And I haven't. You have something I need. You have to help me find John Chapman."

CHAPTER TEN

When Brian Sadler graduated from high school in Longview, Texas and went to Oklahoma University, he had thought about majoring in the subject he found most fascinating - archaeological studies. His father, editor of the local newspaper, had wisely advised him that a major in archaeology might be satisfying and fun but it probably wouldn't pay the bills. Becoming a university instructor would be the likely result of an archaeology degree. Although he would have liked to be another Indiana Jones, more realistically Brian probably would have struggled to find the time and money to get out of the classroom and into the jungle while trying to keep up with the "publish or perish" demands placed on university professors. So he had majored in finance, a subject that ultimately helped him decide to become a stockbroker.

In June before his freshman year at OU the university sent him paperwork asking if he wished to choose his roommate or be randomly matched. Brian had a couple of friends from high school who were also heading north to Norman, Oklahoma, but he decided he wanted to expand his horizons. He didn't want to be around his home-town people and the same old routine. He wanted to make new friends and have new experiences. So he opted for a random match. Within two weeks he received the name of his roommate in a letter from the university. And his father was impressed by the name he read: William Henry Harrison IV from Oklahoma City, Oklahoma.

"Do you know who William Henry Harrison III is?" Brian's father asked him after reading the letter.

"I've heard of him. Isn't he a Senator or something?"

"He is in fact the senior Senator from the state of Oklahoma. He's a great-grandson several times removed of William Henry Harrison, the ninth president and the first to die in office, and also of Benjamin Harrison, our twenty-third president."

Brian's dad was a history buff and he knew his presidents. He went on to point out that Brian's roommate was undoubtedly the Senator's son. At his mother's suggestion, Brian sent Harrison a brief note telling him about himself and saying they'd meet at OU in a few weeks. He got a short note back in an almost illegible script. It said, "Call me Harry. See you soon. Boomer Sooner!"

THE STRANGEST THING

When Brian and his parents arrived at the university on move-in day they found a tall skinny boy standing in Brian's assigned dorm room at Adams Hall, the tower reserved for freshmen. The boy's parents were there too - Brian recognized his roommate's father from pictures Brian's dad had shown him.

"Senator," he said, sticking out his hand, "I'm Brian Sadler. And you must be Harry." Brian and Harry shook hands vigorously.

The boys' mothers introduced themselves and sat on one of the twin beds, talking about how to arrange the tiny room and then making it happen. The ladies had spoken by phone a couple of weeks earlier and had picked sheets and towels that were the same for both boys. This sort of thing mattered more to girls but the moms wanted the guys to at least have some small sense of order in what would otherwise be the chaos of an all-male dormitory.

Senator Harrison and Brian's father went downstairs to the parking lot and helped their sons offload boxes and suitcases. They carried them up three flights of stairs rather than waiting on two banks of elevators that were never available due to the crush of eight hundred boys moving in at the same time.

Harry opened a box packed to the brim with CDs. Brian immediately stopped what he was doing and began looking through the titles.

"I brought a lot too," he told Harry, "but from what I can see we don't have that many duplicates." They talked about their favorite singers and songs. They learned they had both been at the Michael Jackson concert in Dallas six months ago, along with twenty thousand others.

After two hours of unpacking, arranging, and rearranging the mothers declared the project basically finished. "Let's go grab a bite to eat," Senator Harrison said. Brian's parents didn't know Norman at all so they deferred to the legislator's suggestion, a place called Legend's that he said was the best in town. As they waited to be seated several patrons who were leaving spoke to Senator Harrison. He had been an Oklahoma politician for over thirty years, serving first as state Senator, then Governor and now in Washington. He was well known and highly respected by many people in this conservative state.

By midafternoon the boys were dropped back at the dorm. Senator Harrison had to catch a flight to D.C. that evening and Brian's father wanted to get on the road back to Longview. They all expressed enjoyment at meeting and the boys seemed ready for some time to get to know each other away from their parents.

Freshman year went very well for the boys. Although Brian was settled on finance as a major and Harry was interested in political science, their first year was mostly basic courses, pretty much the same for everyone regardless of his ultimate major.

THE STRANGEST THING

By the time summer came around the boys were fast friends, had joined the same fraternity and committed to room together the next year in the frat house. Brian spent that summer working outdoors at an operating cattle ranch in east Texas his grandfather owned and Harry Harrison was in Washington interning for a Congressman from Arizona who was a good friend of his father's. Harry and Brian spent their sophomore and senior years as roommates and best friends. The only break in their collegiate time together was when Harry was selected as a Rhodes scholar and spent his junior year in England. Even then he and Brian corresponded weekly, giving each other the latest information in their lives.

After graduation Harry was accepted at Harvard Law School while Brian landed a job as a stockbroker at Merrill Lynch in Dallas. They stayed in close touch as Harry's career moved up. Harry graduated with honors from law school and returned to Oklahoma City where he was elected a U.S. Representative, the youngest in Oklahoma history. His father retired from the Senate and Harry ran for his seat, winning by a landslide over the Democratic opponent.

While in law school Harry had met a girl named Jennifer Todd who now worked for the Department of the Treasury. It was only natural that Brian Sadler served as his best man at the wedding and as godfather to their first child. They now had two girls and often kidded Brian about when he was going to settle down and marry Nicole Farber, the Dallas lawyer who was now Brian's girlfriend.

Not long thereafter John Chapman became the Republican candidate for President and picked Senator William Henry Harrison IV as his running mate. The election was decided by less than a hundred thousand votes and not until well after midnight. Brian Sadler was in Washington for the watch party at the Willard Hotel. By 3 a.m. only two people remained - Brian and Harry shared a celebratory snifter of brandy in Harry's suite, Secret Service agents standing guard in the hallway and his wife sound asleep in the bedroom next door.

Likewise, Brian was invited to the inauguration and Nicole accompanied him. After a night of dinner and dancing they went back to Harry's home in Georgetown. Soon Harry would move into Number One Observatory Circle, a beautiful place on the grounds of the U.S. Naval Observatory that had served since the 1970s as the residence of the Vice President of the United States. But that move wouldn't happen for about a week so the morning after the inauguration party Brian and Nicole, Harry and Jennifer sat in the den of the Georgetown home having breakfast. They laughed about how close the two men had always been and Brian had said, "You're not going to forget me, are you?"

Brian listened closely as Harry Harrison gave him the few details about President Chapman's disappearance that were not known to the public. "I need you to come down here to Washington tomorrow," the President said,

76

"get fully briefed on everything then go to Palenque and see what you can find."

"Why me, Harry? I'm not a detective. I'm not even an archaeologist. I'm just a guy who dabbles in all that stuff."

"Don't sell yourself short. You're more than a dabbler, Brian. You have a burning interest in Mayan sites like Palenque and you've got a good, intuitive thought process. Most importantly, I trust you implicitly. That last part is more crucial than anything right now. You wouldn't believe some of the strange stories that are circulating around this town. The kooks come out of the woodwork when there's a mystery. The FBI's gotten tips ranging from an ancient curse to Al Qaida to someone thinking he's fallen into a cenote in the jungle. I need to get your input and fast. Every hour that goes by throws this country deeper into confusion. He's somewhere, Brian. I need to know where. The people need to know where."

CHAPTER ELEVEN

Saturday

Nine days after the disappearance

Brian sat in the First Class lounge at Penn Station at 6:15 a.m., ready to catch Amtrak's Acela Express to Union Station in D.C. He'd be in the capital by 9:30 and Harry's appointments secretary had told Brian to watch for FBI agents who would meet him.

The train pulled in to the massive Washington railway station on time. Brian saw two men in black suits approach as he stepped off the train car. "Mr. Sadler, I'm Special Agent Foster," one said. "And this is Special Agent Farmer." They both produced IDs that Brian gave a glance.

"How did you recognize me?"

THE STRANGEST THING

"Sir, that's our job. We have a sedan waiting just outside so please follow us."

They left the station and eventually turned onto the broad expanse of Pennsylvania Avenue. Brian had been to the Visitor's Entrance of the White House several times since Harry became Vice President. This time things were different - the car passed the familiar guardhouse where he had expected to enter and pulled into a driveway further down. Past a security guard and fence there was nothing but what looked like a heavily fortified garage door, which was closed. The agent who was driving showed his credentials to the guard as another with a dog circled the car and looked under it with a mirror. The garage door opened at the same time as the gate – inside Brian could see a ramp heading down.

The car pulled through the gate and down the ramp into an underground parking garage. There were only a dozen cars there, including the armored limousine that the President used. It appeared they were in the Chief Executive's private garage. The sedan pulled forward and stopped where a man in a suit was standing. He opened the rear door and said, "Good morning, Mr. Sadler. I'm Bob Parker, the President's Chief of Staff. Thanks for coming on such short notice." He led Brian through automatic glass doors to a small elevator. They rode up one floor and exited into a narrow hallway. Turning right, they stepped into the President's secretary's office. She introduced herself, wrote a message on her computer and said, "Please go in. The President is waiting for you."

Brian was surprised to see that it appeared to be business as usual even though it was a weekend. *I guess things don't stop just because it's Saturday. Especially when you're running the United States of America.*

Bob Parker ushered Brian through a door into the Oval Office. It was Brian's first time to see the famous room and he found himself a little lightheaded at the experience. "Brian," President Harrison's voice boomed from across the room. "You're a sight for sore eyes!" He came from around his desk and gave Brian a bear hug. "God, I'm glad you came."

Harry Harrison glanced at his Chief of Staff. "Bob, we'll be fine now. Ask Marcia to have some coffee sent in, please."

When they were alone, Brian said, "Uh, Mr. President . . ."

"Dammit, I told you on the phone to knock that off, Brian. I may be 'Mr. President' to everyone else but when it's just us let's try to keep some sense of the normal in our relationship if we can."

"That's a challenge, Harry. I'm not just sitting here shooting the bull with my old fraternity brother from OU. I'm in the Oval Office talking with the President of the United States. I doubt you could ever understand, but it's a very unusual feeling. You're the top dog of the whole world and I'm the guy who knows you wore red panties under your tuxedo to the Christmas Dance at the frat house, just because I bet you twenty bucks you wouldn't do it. This is kind of hard to process in my brain."

"Well, get over it. We'll invite you and Nicole back to D.C. on a lighter occasion sometime soon, I promise. Today we have a lot to talk about and only a few hours to do it. I promised I'd have you on the six o'clock train to Manhattan and I'm trying to keep us on schedule. I'm going to bring some people in to brief you about the situation with President Chapman so you can get a better handle on what we know . . . which sadly is very, very little. Then we're going to strategize on how we can find out more. You're going to hear a lot today, some of it top secret. I've gotten you temporary clearance for this one project."

Except for a half hour break at one p.m. for lunch in a dining room two doors down from the Oval Office, the men worked nonstop until five. The Directors of the National Security Agency, CIA and FBI joined Brian and the President at various times during the afternoon. Much of what Brian learned was public information because, as Harry Harrison had pointed out, there wasn't much else they knew.

Once he and Brian were alone again, Harry turned the conversation to Sussex University and its permit to dig at Palenque. "One important reason I asked you to help, Brian, is that you know Cory Spencer. That connection should help you gather information."

"I didn't know he was involved but I'm not surprised. I've followed his work since he left my gallery.

From what I gather he's making a good archaeologist. I presume he's part of the dig there?"

"Spencer's led several Sussex teams recently and he was handpicked by Thomas Newton Torrance to supervise this one. Speaking of which, what do you know about this character they call TNT?" the President asked.

"I've never met him but I've heard of him like everyone else who reads the news. He seems to make his money robbing from companies to enrich himself but so far he hasn't been convicted of anything. At least as far as I've heard. And about his putting up ten million bucks to back this project - that's commitment."

"You're right. The FBI checked his background, just as we're doing for anyone who's even remotely connected to this story. Torrance has managed to stay clean even though he's a frequent visitor to court and deposition rooms on both sides of the pond. His tactics are questionable for sure but so far no one has proven they're illegal. Had you ever heard before now that he was interested in ancient sites?"

Brian shook his head. "I've never seen his name associated with anything in this field – no sites, no artifacts, nothing. Wonder why he suddenly became so interested in this one particular project that he was willing to fund it for millions? Have your guys talked to him yet?"

"Yes and no. The FBI contacted him and asked for an interview to see if he could give them any clues to

THE STRANGEST THING

President Chapman's disappearance. TNT politely said he was a busy man, had no knowledge of anything he felt would help them and barring a subpoena he wouldn't agree to meet with them. Since the FBI director doesn't have anything he could use to get a subpoena that's pretty much it unless something else turns up."

"Do you think he's trying to hide something?"

"The FBI doesn't see anything worth pursuing, and believe me, they usually think *everyone* is trying to hide something. There's just nothing linking TNT and the former President at all. They've never met, Chapman's records don't show they've ever spoken by phone, and there just doesn't appear to be a connection. So I don't think they'll pursue their attempt to interview him."

"Speaking of that, so you all have records of every phone call the President makes or receives? That might be helpful."

"Not really. We have logs that are supposed to include every call, but there are ways around it. Only calls made through the White House switchboard are logged. And every President in recent history, including me, has a cell phone. Obviously only a handful of people know the number, but we use it to make calls that are private or sensitive. The guys hired to protect us hate it because they don't know what we're up to, but it serves a purpose. For instance, John Chapman used his when he was having an affair. More than one affair, actually."

"I think I read something about that," Brian said. "I guess his wife was aware of his indiscretions."

"I personally have no idea but I figure she must have been. Apparently he's had several affairs; the last one I know about was a few years ago. At least publicly the Chapmans appeared to have moved on so everybody else did too. Not like other presidents haven't stepped out of bounds now and then."

"Any way that latest girlfriend could be involved?"

"The FBI talked with her. Trust me, they're leaving no stone unturned. They say she's not. She went on with her life and is out in California somewhere working in the film industry."

President Harrison changed the subject. "Enough background. I want to get to the real reason I asked you to come today.

"We have all the experts we can handle on this case. The best of the best. Mexico has allowed us to send agents from every damned agency we can think of and no one's found a thing. You know those puzzle things you read about when you're a kid – where a person is in a locked room and dies of a gunshot wound or something, but there's no gun? And you have to figure out the mystery? That's what this reminds me of. It looks like there was no place for John Chapman to go, but he's not there any more. So where is he?

THE STRANGEST THING

"John Chapman has a dark side, Brian. I've seen him tear subordinates to pieces, figuratively speaking of course, in front of a roomful of people when they said or did something he didn't like. He's got a horrible temper. Rumors are that he and Marianne's marriage is a sham but I don't know that for sure. I do know that she sleeps in a different bedroom. Not occasionally, but every night. He's not a nice guy. That's it in a nutshell. He's a cruel, cold, ruthless man who has the money to push his way into anything he wants."

The President continued. "What does all this have to do with Palenque? I have no idea. But in you I have someone I trust implicitly, who's got a brain and knows how to use it, who will travel with the full authority of the President of the United States to ask questions and get answers and who knows enough about archaeology to decide what to look into. I can't figure out what's up, Brian, but we've done everything we can through official channels. I decided to see if you could find out the answer. Maybe you can, maybe you can't. Please go try."

Before ten that evening Brian was back at his apartment in New York. Even on Saturday the train had been packed. Some of the travelers had been working in Washington just like Brian. Others were families, tourists too probably.

On the crowded train he had tried to reach Nicole. Her cellphone went straight to voicemail without ringing; he figured she was at dinner and had turned off her phone. He left a message that he had been in

Washington all day but would call her when he was back in Manhattan.

Arriving home exhausted mentally and physically from the long day, he tried Nicole again with the same result. It was an hour earlier in Dallas so he left a message for her to call if she got home soon. He told her, "I met with Harry today. I'm going to Mexico day after tomorrow as part of the search for President Chapman. I'll fill you in when we talk."

Two days later Brian was in Mexico standing on top of a Mayan ruin, alone. He could see jungle for miles around him. Behind him he heard a noise. He turned and saw President John Chapman ten feet away, wearing the clothes of a priest – a robe and a feathered hat - and holding a scepter. He looked at Brian.

"You have no idea what you're getting into," he said evenly in the ancient Mayan dialect. Brian knew it was Mayan but somehow he understood it clearly.

"Mr. President," Brian said, surprised that his words were also in the Mayan tongue.

"No longer. I am K'inich Janaab Pakal. I am the ruler of Palenque."

As Brian watched, the President's face changed from the one so familiar to every American. It metamorphosed into another face Brian recognized – the one depicted on the lid of King Pakal's coffin. President Chapman was the ancient king.

"Bow to me!" Pakal screamed as a bell began to ding quietly. Brian fell to his knees, his face on the stone floor. He heard the bell ring again and again. Brian looked up and suddenly saw his bedroom ceiling. His cellphone was ringing.

"Uh, Nicole," he stuttered into the phone, confused by the dream from which he had abruptly awoken. Glancing at the clock beside his bed he saw that it was nearly midnight. He was on top of the covers, his naked body sweating profusely. Suddenly freezing, he dived under the covers and pulled the sheet up to his neck.

"Babe. Sorry I missed your call earlier. Big dinner with a big client. You know how it goes."

Brian didn't respond. He was trying to exorcise the dream and focus on reality.

"Hey Brian. Are you ok?"

"Yeah . . . give me a minute. I was asleep. I was dreaming about President Chapman and a Mayan ruin."

"Of course you were, Brian. It would have surprised me a lot more if you were dreaming about me!" She laughed.

"I dream about you all the time. Did you have a good dinner?" His questions were cautious, careful.

"It was good. Mr. Carter had cocktails and dinner with Richard Stewart – have you heard of him? Randall asked me to come along since I had no plans for the evening, as usual. We ate at Sevy's on Preston Road."

"That's one of my favorite restaurants, as you well know. Richard Stewart. The name sounds familiar. Should I know him?"

"He's a patent troll. Or a 'patent assertion entity' if you want to be nice about what he does." She explained that Stewart, an attorney from Las Vegas, started a company and bought up several obscure patents in the technology field from small companies that had no use for them. One of the patents was for a small semiconductor device that was a minor part of the avionics package used by private airplanes.

"Asserting his patent rights, he threatened to sue the suppliers of the avionics, the manufacturers like Beechcraft and Cessna plus the people who bought the planes. Almost all these companies would rather settle than go to court, even if the suit is groundless. Why spend years and millions of dollars fighting when you can pay a hundred thousand now and get a full release?"

Brian responded, trying to shake off sleep and keep up with Nicole's story. He wanted her evening to have been the way she was telling it. "Yeah, I've read about these guys in the Wall Street Journal. They make their money by threatening and settling. They hardly ever end up in court. Everybody hates them – right?"

"Pretty much. Since Rich is an attorney himself he doesn't have to spend any money on outside lawyers, which would otherwise be his biggest expense. Instead he handles everything with a small staff. Brian, he's made over a million bucks in the past twelve months alone. You kind of gotta hate him but gotta love him at the same time. What a racket. And all legal."

"Yeah, but scum of the earth stuff to most people, from what I've read. Nicole, if it's OK can we talk about all this later? I'm going in to work really early tomorrow since I'm going to be gone for a few days."

"Oh sure, baby. I'm sorry. I'm just still pumped up from our dinner but I wanted to talk to you tonight if I could. What's Harry got you doing?"

He told her about the conversation with President Harrison. "He said to tell you we're invited to the White House soon and sent his regards." Brian said he would be catching a government jet from Teterboro Airport in New Jersey. "I don't know why he thinks I can help but he wants me to go to Palenque and nose around. You know how much I love going to the jungle. I hope I can help Harry but I'm also glad to be going back to Mexico."

"I'm certain of that, Brian. I'm a little surprised though - I thought you were really busy at work. You know I wanted you to fly down here to Dallas last weekend but you said you had too much going on at the gallery . . ."

89

"Nicole," he said with a sinking feeling in his heart. "I want to see you every chance I can. But I hope you understand this involves a request from the President of the United States . . ."

"No need to explain, sweetie," she replied breezily. "Hey, look at the time. I'll let you get back to sleep - I'll be nodding off myself shortly. Talk to you soon – call me often while you're gone, baby, and let me know you're ok."

"Wait a sec. Are you ok with all this? And was dinner tonight like you just told me it was? With Randall Carter and that client?" *Damn.* He regretted blurting that last sentence. It wasn't part of their agreement.

"I'm fine, Brian. I know you'd cancel a lunch with the Pope to go exploring in the jungle. I know where everything fits in. And no, I didn't lie to you although you shouldn't ask. It was just another business dinner. Nothing more. No problem here! 'Night, sweetie."

"I love you, Nicole. Good night."

Brian lay in bed, wide-awake. He thought about Nicole and her frequent dinners with her divorced boss, Randall Carter, and the firm's clients. He felt more than a twinge of jealousy. She was a beautiful woman and over a thousand miles away from him. She seemed to enjoy the social part of business more and more lately. Why had she hung up without responding to his "I love you?" She hadn't said anything at all. What did that mean? He forced his mind to stop racing to these crazy conclusions.

Nicole was the youngest partner in Dallas' premier law firm. She specialized in white-collar criminal defense work and that was how she and Brian Sadler had met. When he was a stockbroker for Warren Taylor and Currant, an investment bank that played close to the edge on matters of ethics and integrity, he found himself embroiled in a case the FBI was investigating. Nicole acted first as his attorney but the business relationship had quickly turned into a personal one. Once Brian assumed control of Bijan Rarities and moved to Manhattan he knew they were destined to be apart. Her career was in Texas while his was with his gallery in New York and his new location in London.

Although separated by fifteen hundred miles and diverging career paths, Brian and Nicole saw each other as often as one of them could break away. Marriage had never been seriously discussed – a long distance marriage was the only thing either of them could think of that was worse than a long distance relationship.

He really wished it could be different. They met as often as they could – a weekend here, an overseas trip there – but with the situation they couldn't live in the same place. Originally they had agreed to exclusively see each other but recently Nicole had broached a subject that had been in the backs of their minds.

The last time they were together had been in Dallas. Lying in bed in her condominium at the Ritz-

Carlton Residences Nicole had said, "This is mentally and physically draining, Brian." She was referring to their long-distance relationship and asked Brian if there were anyone he would consider dating if he were free.

"Not at all," he responded curtly. "You?"

"Nope, and that's why now's a good time to talk. I'm not suggesting we do a single thing differently about each other. I love you, Brian, but I can't move. You can't move either. So we're long-distance significant others, stealing time when we can, until something changes. I'm not looking for anyone else, even a man to date casually, but I'm a red-blooded American just like you are. Sometime, somewhere a situation may come up where I'd like to have a drink with a guy, maybe even a dinner, and not feel like I'm cheating on you. I think we should see other people if we choose to. When we can figure out how to be together then that'll be the best of all. For now, it sucks."

Although her suggestion deeply disturbed Brian he hid his feelings. He said he agreed. "I doubt I'll be doing that myself," he had said, "but if something comes up then I'll let you know."

"Actually, I think it's better we don't do that. Telling me you're going out is like salt in the wound, don't you think? What we don't know won't make us sad or jealous or wistful. So I don't think we should quiz each other. Let's just work hard to be together as much as possible."

THE STRANGEST THING

"That's all just great," Brian had responded, his voice shaking. "You've just got this all figured out, don't you? It's kind of sad how easily this entire discussion went down for you. But I'm sure you were prepared for this little talk. Just like you always are in the courtroom. Never ask a question you don't know the answer to. Right, Nicole? Isn't that your strategy? Isn't that what makes you a great lawyer?"

The rest of Brian's trip to Dallas had been a strain on them. Since they began dating Nicole's schedule had been rigorous and included long hours both in the office and with clients and lawyers away from work. It was part of her job and rising stars at Carter and Wells were expected to donate their personal time to corporate affairs. It was always frustrating when Brian was at home in New York and couldn't reach Nicole but she explained that she muted her phone during business dinners. She had told him if there ever were something urgent to send her a text twice in one minute and she'd respond as soon as possible.

Now every time Brian couldn't contact Nicole for hours after she'd left the office he had a nagging thought that her proposed plan had started. His mind played tricks – he saw her sitting in a bar in Highland Park Village having a drink with a new friend, or at a steakhouse in Addison sharing wine and dinner with someone who could eventually take Brian's place in her bed . . . or her heart.

BILL THOMPSON

CHAPTER TWELVE

Sunday

Ten days after the disappearance

The question of the fate of the missing American president went unanswered as days passed with absolutely no word. But another mystery could be kept under wraps no longer.

The Secretary of State sat in the Oval Office with President Harrison and Chief of Staff Bob Parker. The Secretary had received a call from his counterpart in Mexico, the Foreign Secretary. The three men listened to the recorded conversation.

"Mr. Secretary, I want to advise that we intend to release the story of the discovery at Palenque today. We regret that your President's whereabouts are still unknown but our government feels after ten days it is deceptive if we continue to ignore the questions people are asking."

Two days before the FBI had reluctantly concluded its search of the rooms deep inside the temple. Lacking permission from the Mexican authorities for an invasive search of the chambers' walls and floors there was nothing more to be done. Once they left the Mexican government sent a team of archaeologists and scientists to examine the mysterious artifact that lay in the newly discovered room below King Pakal's tomb. As more people saw the object it became impossible to keep it a secret. The Mexican government risked being accused of a cover-up if a press release wasn't forthcoming quickly.

President Harrison thought for a moment about what the Secretary had told him. "Frankly I'm surprised they haven't broken the story before now. I have no idea what that thing is down there – from the pictures I've seen it looks like some kind of strut to support something – but it definitely is in a place it shouldn't be. Who would have buried what looks like a modern piece of metal deep inside a temple over five hundred years ago? And what the hell is it?"

"Sir, my understanding is the archaeologists intend to bring the artifact out of the temple and examine it in a laboratory environment. Up to this point, no one has been allowed to touch or move it. From the pictures it looks like it's just sitting on the stone altar so theoretically it'd be no problem to bring it to the surface."

THE STRANGEST THING

On the other side of the Atlantic Ocean Thomas Newton Torrance was having a late lunch in the restaurant of the Ritz Hotel on Piccadilly in the heart of London. He loved the ambiance of what many called the most beautiful dining experience in the world. And he enjoyed the service. As a very frequent guest and an extravagant tipper, TNT garnered the admiration and envy of staff and diners alike. His table by the window was always available for him. On the frequent occasion when the restaurant was full for lunch TNT's venue was still held until last in the event he showed up without a reservation. One day he had strolled in when the restaurant was packed solid. Without batting an eyelash the maître d' ushered TNT into the adjoining bar for a quick complimentary champagne while a party of four was summarily uprooted from TNT's spot. A hastily erected table became the foursome's new lunch venue. Although it was inconvenient the diners, who turned out to be American tourists, were thrilled once they heard whose table they had occupied. Everyone knew the name Thomas Newton Torrance, the bad boy billionaire. He was as well known as Donald Trump and the tourists had a great story for friends and family back home . . . plus a free three hundred dollar lunch compliments of the Ritz.

Torrance read The Evening Standard newspaper as he sipped a glass of his current favorite wine, Domaine Leflaive Puligny-Montrachet. At around $700 a bottle, each glass drained nearly $200 from Torrance's net worth. But his various investments and corporate activities added far more than that every minute so things were fine for

Thomas Newton Torrance and his penchant for the best of everything.

He felt a vibration in the inside pocket of his suit jacket and glanced surreptitiously at the screen without removing the phone. Cell phones were absolutely forbidden in the dining room. Even a guest of his caliber would be admonished for texting or even looking at the screen. A ringing phone would get you quickly ushered to the door, regardless of your status. It just wasn't done.

He pushed his chair back and a waiter rushed over to assist. "I'll be right back," he said, heading to the lobby. The waiter brought a clean napkin and carefully folded it to await TNT's return.

In the lobby outside the restaurant TNT looked at his phone. Two words had been texted – *call me*. He hit a number in his contacts list and soon heard the international ring tone. When the call connected, TNT listened to Cory Spencer for five minutes.

Torrance's voice trembled. "That complicates matters. Say nothing to anyone about this – do you understand? I'll be there as quickly as I can." Torrance's hands were visibly shaking as he ended the call. His heart was racing and he felt lightheaded. A porter in the hallway walked toward him to see if he was all right. TNT waved him off and paused to regain his composure.

Before returning to the restaurant he called his travel agent who as always dropped everything for her most important client. The commission on his first class tickets bought the agent a lavish lifestyle. Torrance booked a British Airways flight for the next day from London's Heathrow Airport to Mexico City. He'd be there by late afternoon tomorrow.

As he finished lunch, Torrance reflected for a moment on the good old days when he could have caught the afternoon Concorde from London to New York, arriving in just over three hours instead of the usual six or seven, then connected anywhere he wished that same evening. He could have been in Mexico City tonight, but those times were gone so he was forced to fly the slower way – albeit in first class. He could fly private, of course. He did that a lot but not for transatlantic flights. He had weighed the cost and convenience and even with money to burn he decided to burn it somewhere other than on jet fuel.

As he finished lunch, TNT made notes on a small pad he took from his pocket. The call from Cory Spencer in Palenque had given him three important pieces of information. The first was that the artifact was coming to the surface for examination – it was news Torrance was waiting to hear and it meant he had to get to Palenque as quickly as possible. Immediately.

The second bit of information was amazing - it made his heart race. Cory told Torrance there was more to see than just the artifact in its chamber. He had found something else. It was something that for years TNT had remotely considered might be possible but now perhaps it was true. The thought was so mind-boggling he could scarcely imagine how significant it could be to the entire world.

Cory had told him one last thing, something that had happened. The news was devastating. It could undermine everything Torrance had spent ten million dollars to accomplish. This news was so monumental that for once the brilliant Thomas Newton Torrance didn't have any idea what to do. He hadn't considered this possibility. He forced himself to put it aside for now. The time to deal with this was when he arrived in Mexico; there was nothing he could do from here and there were other things to handle first.

He needed to call Dr. Armando Ortiz at the Archaeological Institute in Mexico City, the man who was directing the plan to bring the artifact out of its chamber for examination. When that happened Torrance was going be present. He had paid ten million dollars to fund the Palenque project and the object had been found thanks to his donation. He had also personally ensured his new friend Dr. Ortiz had access to even more money both for his personal endeavors and for future digs – something Mexico desperately wanted.

In return for the financial assistance from Torrance, Dr. Ortiz had so far been extremely responsive to the entrepreneur's requests. And this time would be no exception. TNT would be there to observe the artifact's examination. Period.

The same way he had been in the chamber just after the artifact was discovered.

THE STRANGEST THING

Thomas Newton Torrance was certain he would have access to everything the archaeologists knew. He just didn't know yet how he would see what Cory Spencer had found – the strangest thing.

CHAPTER THIRTEEN
Monday
Eleven days after the disappearance

Thomas Newton Torrance jotted notes as he reclined in his first class seat. The British Airways flight would arrive in Mexico City in a little under four hours. From there he had arranged a twin Cessna turboprop to fly him to Palenque airport.

From the moment he heard Cory's news Torrance had struggled with the information the dig supervisor had given him. With difficulty Torrance had maintained his composure and stifled first excitement then terror as he stood in the lobby of the Ritz listening to Cory's revelations. The archaeologist had told him both a monumental secret and the single most amazing thing TNT had ever heard. It was also so far-fetched that

THE STRANGEST THING

Torrance had only dreamt it might be the answer to many mysteries. Now it seemed it was true!

But Cory's bombshell changed all that. As he listened to Cory's third revelation on the phone yesterday, TNT's exhilaration had changed to fear, then hatred for the archaeologist, all in a matter of moments. Torrance forced himself to rationally think through the implications of Cory's final disclosure. Why had the archaeologist waited ten days to explain to Torrance what happened the day the President disappeared? Torrance been certain Cory knew something that day. Not only had President Chapman gone missing, Cory Spencer himself had been mysteriously absent for the entire day.

Why is this happening? My greatest triumph. Undoubtedly the most significant thing man has ever discovered on earth. Why is it all in jeopardy now? Torrance forced the negative thoughts out of his mind. He was experienced in the art of focusing on what was important – what he could control – and putting the rest aside.

The first thing TNT had to do was figure out how to get down into the chamber alone with Cory Spencer. Dr. Ortiz would be reticent but it would happen. Once he saw for himself what the dig leader had found Torrance could decide the next move. As long as Cory could be kept quiet the secret would remain hidden for as long as Torrance wanted. Unless someone else discovered the secret he'd come across. Or if Cory decided to break confidence. *That would be unwise,* Torrance thought idly. He wasn't stupid enough to risk everything for such a move. *I'll kill him myself if this gets screwed up*. That wouldn't happen, of course. Thomas Newton Torrance never did his own dirty work. There were other people for those kinds of chores.

The entrepreneur sipped a glass of Bollinger champagne – not his favorite but not bad for an airline choice either. Why had Cory picked yesterday to tell Torrance what he knew? Had he just found all this out himself? Or had he known it for days? TNT had questions that needed answering – he would deal with this archaeologist face-to-face very soon.

CHAPTER FOURTEEN
Tuesday
Twelve days after the disappearance

In Palenque preparations were underway to bring the ancient artifact to the surface. With nothing to report about the missing leader for almost two weeks, the world had begun to lose interest. As dramatic as his disappearance had been, in an era of instant news people had started to move on to other things. If he were found then interest would revive. For now the subject had become yesterday's news.

Now there was something interesting going on. Permission to televise the artifact's removal had been granted to only two sources: Aguascalientes TV, the Mexican government's network, and the US-based Fox News. Both had set up satellite trucks in the parking lot several hundred yards away. Commentators stood in the plaza between the Palace and the Temple of the Inscriptions.

This was a very exciting day for the world. Up to this point the government had allowed a drawing of the artifact to be released to the news agencies but no one had seen a real picture of it. Speculation abounded as to what it was. Everyone seemed to have a different opinion and a lot of people were anxious to see what it really looked like.

Thomas Newton Torrance had arrived in Palenque yesterday afternoon. He arranged for a driver to take him to the hotel his travel agent had recommended. Although he preferred the amenities of a luxury hotel chain, this place had pleasantly surprised him. The tiny boutique property was a refreshing change. It was situated in the jungle on the road to the ruins, had a decent wine list and tolerable food. He was satisfied with La Casa Hermosa.

Torrance had unsuccessfully tried to get in touch with Cory Spencer. The archaeologist didn't answer his cellphone and wasn't at the crew barracks, a structure that the government maintained not far from the archaeological grounds for the use of visiting dig teams. Angry at Spencer's obvious avoidance, TNT decided to bide his time. Cory would turn up eventually.

And he did. In the room at the summit of the Temple of the Inscriptions three men stood while the news team waited for permission to scale the temple steps and join them. Dr. Ortiz, director of the National

THE STRANGEST THING

Institute of Archaeology and History, talked quietly with Cory. Standing next to them reading a message on his cell phone was Thomas Newton Torrance. Despite the jungle heat and humidity, Torrance was dressed in a tan three-piece linen suit and Hermes tie.

Torrance had first seen Cory when the entrepreneur arrived at the temple that morning. He pulled Spencer aside, roughly taking his arm. Cory jerked away.

"Where have you been?" TNT whispered angrily.

"Mr. Torrance, I didn't know exactly when you were coming. I've been attending to several things. I hope you don't think I was purposely avoiding you. Why would I do that? After all, if I hadn't called, you wouldn't be here right now."

The archaeologist's blasé attitude made Torrance furious. "Listen to me, you little . . ." His voice rose slightly and Dr. Ortiz glanced over.

"Is everything all right, senores?"

"Of course," Torrance replied. "We were just discussing the exciting things happening this morning." He looked at Cory and whispered through clenched teeth, "I'll deal with you later."

Ortiz said, "All right, then. I think it's time to start the program."

The plan was for the Aguascalientes newscaster to go down the stone staircase to Pakal's cramped tomb and shoot camera footage into the chamber below. Viewers everywhere would watch as two archaeologists wrapped the artifact and lifted it up to be carried to the top of the stairway. Fox would simultaneously pick up that camera footage from its vantage point outside the temple.

Everything began just fine. At exactly ten a.m. the team descended the stairway and the broadcast began. People around the world tuned in to the show. They followed the camera down the stone stairs until the sarcophagus of King Pakal came into view. All the protective covering had been removed so the viewers could see the remarkable coffin lid in its splendor. The strange drawing of the king lying on his back, hands on what some people thought looked like aircraft controls, added to the mystery of what lay below.

The newscasters spoke in Spanish and English as the camera recorded the archaeologists descending the ladder into the newly discovered chamber below Pakal's tomb. They focused on the object itself. Its dented, mangled surface shone with a dull gleam as millions of people saw the eight-foot-long artifact for the first time. The reporters explained that although it had been underground for at least hundreds of years, the object appeared to be something modern. It was crumpled and damaged but looked like it could be a part from some current machine.

The two archaeologists stood on either side of the artifact and prepared to lift it for the first time. Cameras rolling, they put their gloved hands beneath the object and attempted to raise it up. Nothing happened. The object didn't budge. It was as though it was bolted to the rock slab on which it lay. After ten minutes of trying they gave up.

With no story to report, the news networks quickly shifted back to their studios and to plan B. Archaeologists showed a detailed cross-section of the Temple of the Inscriptions. The structure was nearly eighty feet high – from a room at the top the stone staircase descended all the way to ground level, where Pakal's tomb was. They explained that the room containing the sarcophagus had been built first and the massive temple had been constructed afterwards. There was no debate about that.

What *was* subject to debate was the next thing the archaeologists revealed. From the cross-section they showed, they peeled away a paper that covered the area below Pakal's tomb. This revealed the new chamber that had been found underneath the room where King Pakal's body lay. This was the place where the artifact lay on its stone altar.

A diverse panel had been put together. It ran the gamut from scientists to ancient astronaut theorists and there was heated debate on the object and its purpose. They speculated whether it was ancient or modern – the scientists lost that discussion because there was no reasonable explanation how the artifact could have been placed where it was in recent times. Nobody won the discussions on what it was, where it came from or how long it had been there. Nobody had any idea.

No one on the panel could dispute that the room was at least the same age as King Pakal's tomb, over fifteen hundred years old. Most assumed that it had to be much older. Perhaps the inhabitants of Palenque had found it and Pakal had decided to build his own tomb on top as a symbol of reverence to the unknown gods who may have put the artifact there.

The rest of the broadcast offered background into the Mayan civilization and the settlement at Palenque. *It's a good thing the people at least got to see the artifact,* Dr. Ortiz thought to himself as the camera crews on site at the temple dismantled their equipment. The National Institute director had been as disappointed as the rest to learn that the two men couldn't move the object. Turned out it wasn't affixed to the stone slab at all – it was just incredibly heavy. For the time being the artifact would remain in place. Examining it in situ was going to be a challenge because of the limited space in the chamber. Ortiz figured that no more than three people could easily work in the room at a time due both to space constraints and because fresh air had to be pumped into the chamber continually. He would have to develop a plan about what to do next.

Once the news people had left Thomas Newton Torrance pulled Dr. Ortiz aside and said he wanted to see the artifact. He looked at Cory Spencer and said, "Come with me."

THE STRANGEST THING

Ortiz prepared to join them but Torrance said, "Doctor, we all know I'm a layman. I know nothing about archaeology and you're the expert, but if you'll indulge me I'd like to see the artifact quietly. I'll take Cory because I know you archaeologists don't trust me down there alone with it. He can make sure I don't touch anything I shouldn't!"

Torrance laughed and Ortiz gave a nervous chuckle. He felt he should go with TNT but had been caught off guard, unable to assert himself. It was a function of Torrance's vast wealth – he felt subservient to the British millionaire even though Ortiz had final say over the entire operation at Palenque. Then there was the personal aspect - Ortiz had seen for himself how TNT rewarded those who were on his side. The director's salary was not large. Torrance had already made sure the archaeological director had some extra American dollars – quite a few, truth be told. So Dr. Ortiz let them go alone. He nervously paced the room atop the temple as he awaited their return.

This actually was the second time TNT had gone inside the newly discovered chamber - but only he and Cory Spencer knew that.

As they descended the staircase Cory appeared nervous. He said, "Mr. Torrance, do you want to see the secret passage now . . ."

"Shut up!" TNT whispered. "Voices carry very well up and down this stairway. We'll talk in the chamber." They skirted Pakal's sarcophagus and crawled down the ladder into the newly discovered room where the artifact lay.

By now Cory was visibly shaking. "Mr. Torrance, we need to talk about the passage I found. You told me not to talk about it but I need some help here. I told you about this because I'm going to be famous – my career will skyrocket. We have to plan how to disclose the discovery. This could be the most important thing ever found, maybe. And I'll be famous . . . you too, of course," he added almost as an afterthought. "But we have to figure out what to do about . . . you know. The other thing."

Torrance abruptly changed the subject. "Where were you on the day the President disappeared? I called and texted you a dozen times. No response. What were you doing that afternoon?"

"I had some thinking to do."

"Really? What *thinking* did you have to do, Cory, right here in Palenque on the very afternoon the world went crazy trying to figure out where the President was? That just doesn't make sense. Unless you were involved. Were you involved, Cory?"

"Involved with what? With what happened to the President? No way. It was an . . . I mean, there was nothing I could have done . . ." His eyes darted around the room as he responded.

THE STRANGEST THING

Torrance's voice was hard. "Cory, you owe me some explanations. I know plenty about you and you *will* do what I say. Now's not the time but I want an answer about where you were that afternoon. As far as the passage you found, and the President, that has to wait for now. Until I say it's time. Understand? I'm going to ask you this one more time. Who else knows about this? Only the two of us?" He looked Cory Spencer in the eyes. "Or have you told someone else? Now's the time to tell the truth, Cory. If I find out you lied your life will be . . . Well," the entrepreneur smiled cruelly. "Let's just say your life won't be worth much if you haven't told me everything."

"No, sir. I promise. I swear to you I told no one else but you. But I could . . . uh, I could lose my job over this. And a lot more, if we don't plan this right." He averted his eyes as his body gave an involuntary shudder.

"Lose your *job?* Yes, Cory, you could lose your job and a great deal more. How about your freedom? Or your life? You *need* me, Cory. Far more than I need you. Keep that in mind."

Torrance noticed the change in the man's demeanor. Spencer was scared. He had to handle the archaeologist carefully. Cory knew a lot – until Torrance became privy to it he couldn't alienate him. He decided to move to another subject. They had very little time to talk and he needed answers to several things.

"How long have you known about the passage and the President?"

"Uh, well only a couple of days, Mr. Torrance. I discovered it right before I called you . . ."

TNT figured Cory was lying about the timing. But he had to be careful.

"I want to see the passageway when the time is right, not when people are all around us. No one can know about it until I see where it leads and what else is there. I can afford to wait, Cory. This could be the most important thing ever discovered. You will wait until we have a safe time to open the passage. We'll see it together. We'll be the first to learn what secrets this place holds. Until then you will not go back into the passageway yourself and you will not discuss it. I will not tell you this again - do you understand?"

Cory stammered an affirmation. "But what about the President . . ."

"Cory, you've created a world of problems for yourself. All this on top of the other problem you already had. The one you've *always* had. I'm the only person on earth who can keep you out of trouble. My resources are limitless. I can make virtually anything happen. Good or bad. You and I are going to work together. As a team. The matter of the President is mine to handle. And for now we're going to leave it alone."

Torrance was good with words. Even if they meant nothing, as was the case now. He would use Cory Spencer as long as he needed him. Then the archaeologist would meet with an unfortunate accident and be out of Torrance's life.

Once he knew they weren't going into the hidden hallway Cory's countenance changed and he seemed to relax. Torrance noticed relief on the archaeologist's face. *Cory's bought himself some time,* Torrance thought to himself. *Not much, but I'll give him a little time.*

The archaeologist had taken a calculated risk revealing what he had discovered. Once he knew the artifact was going to be brought to the surface he figured it was only a matter of time until someone else found the hidden passageway. The method to open the corridor was so obscure, so challenging that it was unlikely someone would stumble upon it. *But I did,* Cory thought. *And I want the glory for this one. I wanted it from the very second I saw what's in there. Thomas Newton Torrance isn't taking this away from me. I can deal with him if I have to. I fixed things once before in my life and I can do it again.*

He shuddered at that last statement. He wasn't like that and he had spent a lifetime running away from his past. But he knew it was still in there somewhere. *So TNT had better watch his step with me.*

"Finished daydreaming?" Torrance looked him in the eyes. "You told me the truth about the hidden passage, right? You didn't go all the way to the other end yourself, did you? What are you not telling me?"

"No, sir. I told you the truth. I found out how to open it then . . . then, well, you know . . . the thing with

115

the President, so I closed it and told you about it. I haven't done another thing. I swear, Mr. Torrance. I've told you everything."

Sweat poured off Cory's brow as he attempted to keep his body from shaking. Lying didn't come easily but now he had a problem. He had to find a way out of this. He'd figure out something, with or without this pompous asshole Englishman's help.

"Cory, for your sake I had better never find out you lied to me. I'll protect you as long as I trust you. But if you lied . . ."

Spencer struggled to show a calm, confident face. "I'm telling the truth, Mr. Torrance. I saw there was a room at the end of the passageway but I swear I didn't go there."

"I trust you, Cory." Torrance had to keep him dangling at the moment. It was too dangerous to open the passageway now while Dr. Ortiz was only seventy feet above. At any time he could descend the stone steps and find them. He and Cory would have to come back when they could be alone. That would be hard to arrange but TNT would figure it out.

"I hope you feel I've compensated you well for all you've done so far. Finding the secret passage was good work and look at the bonus you got just for that one thing. A year ago you didn't even know numbered bank accounts existed. Now as of yesterday you have one. There's much more to be learned here. Concentrate on your job. You're my man on the scene. You need to keep passing information to me and me only – no one else. This will all work out. I'll deal with everything when the time is right. You just think about this - you're going to be very wealthy, Cory, if this artifact in front of us is what I believe it is."

Cory agreed with Torrance on this one. He knew what the artifact was, and it was in fact going to make him very wealthy. And famous.

TNT touched the mangled, dirty metallic object. It was ice cold even though the humid room was a stuffy eighty degrees Fahrenheit.

"So what do you think it is?" Cory changed the subject.

Torrance glared at him. "I'm not one to engage in idle speculation about what this is. You shouldn't either. Mind your own business, Cory. You're your own worst enemy. If you do something to screw this up things will go bad in a hurry for you. Worse in fact than you can possibly imagine."

A flash of anger crossed Cory Spencer's face then quickly vanished. Deferentially he said, "Yes sir, you've already told me that. I know how important this is. You can count on me. And I won't breathe a word about anything." Trying again to change the subject he said, "Have your people figured out what it's made of?"

Torrance sighed. He didn't want to deal with this idiot but he had to have the archaeologist in order to accomplish his own goals. "You know how hard this metal was when we tried to flake off a sample the last time we were here. All I had to work with was the pictures I took with my phone. The chemist I consulted is convinced it's iridium but it'll take a sample to be certain."

"Iridium? I've never heard of it."

"I hadn't either," TNT replied, leaving it at that. He had no intention of telling Cory Spencer what he knew.

Torrance's scientific team in England had told him a lot about iridium. It is the densest element on earth and one of the rarest. It occurs in very small quantities on our planet but much, much higher in meteors and asteroids. Many in the scientific community therefore believe iridium is not natural to earth. The scientists had told TNT that very high levels of iridium were found in one particular layer below the surface in eastern Mexico. Many believed the element was deposited there when an asteroid hit the Yucatan peninsula 65 million years ago, a catastrophic event which likely caused the sudden extermination of the dinosaurs from the earth.

The possibility that this metallic object was made of iridium raised two intriguing questions: just how ancient might it be and where did it come from. In his mind TNT had played with the thought that the artifact could be older than the dinosaurs and may not have originated on this planet. If that were true, this would be the rarest object ever found. And it would be priceless.

From his jacket pocket TNT pulled out a small instrument that looked like the remote control for a television. He turned it on and ran it over the surface of the artifact. The machine began to buzz as a needle on a screen moved all the way from left to right.

"It's definitely radioactive," Torrance commented as he turned off the Geiger counter and stuck it in his pocket. "My consultants suggested checking it for radioactivity. Iridium is radioactive for only a very short time. This artifact has been lying on this altar for centuries. That's a fact that's indisputable given where it's situated below Pakal's tomb. If this object is still radioactive and if it's also made of iridium then it's a variation of the element scientists haven't seen before. At least on earth."

"At least on *earth?* Are you suggesting . . ." Cory knew exactly what he was suggesting and he knew how close to the truth the entrepreneur likely was.

"I'm not suggesting anything."

"Sorry, Mr. Torrance. I'm just wondering . . ."

Torrance's words were clipped, uttered through clenched teeth. He was furious. "Shut up, Cory, for God's sake. You talk too much. But I know you'll never tell anything about the things you've found here. Isn't that right, Cory, or should I say Paul? If I ever find out you've breathed a word about this discovery things will go very, very badly for you. You and I both know if your past is revealed you'll lose everything. You'll never work again, except maybe making furniture in a prison workshop. There's no statute of limitations for a person who does what you did."

Cory angrily stared at him, teeth clenched. He forced himself to be quiet. *I'll kill this bastard.*

TNT smiled cruelly. *He hates me as much as I hate him.*

"All right then, Cory. Your secrets are safe with me. And because I hold your fate in my hands, my secrets are safe with you. Keep it that way and you'll be fine. No one will know what you really are. Or what you've hidden."

Torrance turned and started up the stairs. Cory walked behind him with an attitude of subservience. They joined the others in the room at the top of the Temple of the Inscriptions.

"Is everything good?" Dr. Ortiz asked anxiously as Torrance emerged from the stairway. "Did you learn anything new?"

"No. I didn't even touch the artifact – right, Cory?" He smiled at the archaeologist who nodded his head. "I just wanted some time to take it all in. To be

THE STRANGEST THING

there with the object, observe it, wonder about it. I appreciate your allowing that, Dr. Ortiz."

CHAPTER FIFTEEN

The man called Cory Spencer was a twenty-six year old graduate student pursuing an advanced degree in archaeological studies at the prestigious Sussex University in Pennsylvania. Born Paul Emerson and raised in El Paso, Texas, the boy had had a tragic past.

He hadn't started out wanting to be an archaeologist. To be honest, Paul hadn't started out as much of anything. He struggled in school and barely managed to pass even the early grades. At home his father, frustrated at never being sober enough to hold a job for long, exploded in a drunken rage almost every night. His mother and sister took the brunt of the punishing abuse - verbal, physical and emotional - that his father inflicted upon them.

The boy usually managed to duck and swerve, avoiding most of the swings his father dealt with fists and furniture. Sadly, his eight-year-old sister wasn't agile. She had been born with a clubfoot, putting her father into a violent outburst from the moment she arrived. He constantly spewed venom, calling her a useless cripple, his cruel words causing the child to whimper and cry. "Stand up and take it," the man would yell, kicking her as she lay curled up on the floor.

Paul Emerson was eleven years old and in the sixth grade on the day it all ended. He had been in a fight at school that afternoon just like so many other times, and he ended up being on suspension for five days. Suspension didn't help anything. Paul couldn't learn anyway. He was very bright but his mind was filled with hatred, confusion and fear. Counselors and teachers had given up on him. His parents never came to teacher conferences. No one cared so Paul fell through the cracks.

On the last horrible night they were at the dinner table. Paul's father suddenly screamed at his mother about the meal she had fixed. He threw his plate and hit her in the face, hot gravy scalding her skin as the plate shattered into a thousand pieces on the floor. Something snapped in Paul Emerson's head. He didn't remember the dinner knife he had in his hand as he came around the table. He never replayed in his head what happened, so he never recalled exactly how he managed to overpower his father with nothing but the knife. The coroner said it likely started with the old man's eyes. Paul had gone for them first to incapacitate him. Then he had stabbed and stabbed, hundreds of times, until the man died on the kitchen floor.

Paul lay next to his father's body, exhausted but relieved that the ordeal was over for his mother. Then he watched as she fell on her husband's body, sobbing and holding him. Paul stared, amazed at her grief. Was she sorry this monster had finally been stopped? His mother looked at him and screamed, "Why? Why? You'll die in prison for this. They'll kill you. You murdered your own father. How are we going to live? Get out! Get out! I never want to see you again. Get out of here!"

And eleven-year-old Paul Emerson did exactly that.

Paul had several things going for him. He was smart and crafty, could work well with his hands, and was a surprisingly good communicator. He was also tall, lean and handsome. The best thing was that he looked much older than he was. Nobody who saw him had a clue this boy wasn't even a teenager.

He hitchhiked or walked, spending the nights in barns and under bridges as he made his way north. He didn't have a plan and had no idea where he was going. All he knew was he couldn't stay in Texas. He didn't know if the authorities would arrest an eleven-year-old for murder. He didn't know if they would put him on death row and execute him once he turned eighteen. He also didn't care. He was glad he had done what he did.

The first thing Paul Emerson did was to shed the name his father and mother had given him. He picked

THE STRANGEST THING

Cory Spencer – there was nothing special about it. He just wanted a new name and that one sounded ok.

He made his way northeast to Dallas then Tulsa and onwards, doing odd jobs and taking his pay in cash. He didn't have a Social Security number or a bank account so the employment options were few. He washed dishes, joined a roofing crew, helped serve at a Salvation Army soup kitchen – whatever there was to do, he did it.

When he finally ended up on the streets of New York, Cory discovered another way to make money. There he figured out that women – and men too, for that matter – would buy his youthful body for an hour of pleasure. It was easy money. All he had to do was perform well and he could make two or three hundred dollars quickly. It wasn't what he preferred but it bought a place to stay and food to eat. That beat sleeping under a bridge like he had done at first.

One of his patrons was quite wealthy, thirty-something and divorced. Caroline Tipton met Cory as he delivered pizza to her Upper East Side home one evening. Playing out a fantasy she had done many times before, Caroline had answered the door in a see-through negligee. She invited him in and they spent the night together. That started a long relationship. As they got more comfortable with each other, she began to peel away the secrets and learn about Cory's past. Not about Paul Emerson – that person no longer existed. Cory Spencer had his own story and she bought it hook, line and sinker.

He was fifteen years old when he met Caroline Tipton but his appearance allowed him to tell her he was nineteen. He said his mother and father had been killed in a car accident in California and he was sent to live with an aunt who didn't want him, so he took off. He had missed several years of school and had lived on his own, doing whatever he could.

Caroline's interest in the boy went further than the sexual escapades they shared. She saw his potential and she had the money to help him. Cory couldn't have hoped for a luckier break than meeting Caroline Tipton. She set him up in an efficiency apartment in Chelsea and paid a small fortune to create a birth certificate for him. That allowed Cory Spencer to get a Social Security card and a driver's license.

Caroline put him in an academy with both a remedial and an accelerated learning program. The curriculum was designed to bring along those who were behind and allow those who could push ahead to do so. It was perfect. He learned so quickly that he advanced two grades in less than nine months.

By this time Cory was becoming less interesting to Caroline Tipton as a sex toy – she thrived on new things and she found one boy after another to satisfy her desires. But there was something different about Cory Spencer. She felt something for him she didn't know existed in her psyche. Maybe it was love. Or maybe compassion. She was surprised to discover a new feeling - she actually *cared* for the boy she had rescued. So Caroline Tipton stuck with Cory. She paid his exorbitant tuition and his rent and helped him every way she could.

Cory graduated with a high school diploma and Caroline got him a job with an acquaintance of hers. She had made several expensive purchases from a Fifth Avenue antiquities gallery called Bijan Rarities over the past few years and became friends with its owner, Brian Sadler. Sadler needed a general backroom guy. He was pleased to fill the position and accommodate a good client at the same time.

Because the gallery had millions of dollars in rarities in house, potential employees were subjected to a background check including a fingerprint search through the New York Police Department's database. Cory held his breath for ten days – this would be the most likely chance in his life that the truth about his past would be revealed.

He relaxed when Collette Conning, Brian Sadler's assistant, called at last to confirm the job was his. He had successfully transformed himself from Paul Emerson into Cory Spencer. His future was now secure.

Cory worked at Bijan Rarities for four years while he pursued a bachelor's degree at NYU. He was a fast learner and soon had risen from glorified janitor to a valuable post. He was put in charge of cataloging items the gallery received on consignment. He had a particular interest in the ancient pieces from Egypt, Mesopotamia and the Americas. Because of his work at Bijan, Cory chose archaeology as his major and graduated with honors.

Brian Sadler was sorry to lose Cory when he was accepted at Sussex University in Pennsylvania as a graduate student in archaeological studies. Cory had been a good employee and Brian was certain he had a great future ahead of him given the young man's intense interest in antiquities.

Cory Spencer had totally buried Paul Emerson, the juvenile who had murdered his own father. Like a phoenix rising from the ashes, a new person had emerged in the killer's stead. He no longer had to live with the underlying fear he would be found out and imprisoned. And no one was the wiser.

Almost no one.

CHAPTER SIXTEEN

Several years ago, Thomas Newton Torrance, already a successful corporate raider, had heard the rumors of what might lie deep inside the Temple of the Inscriptions at Palenque. For decades people had speculated on King Pakal's mysterious sarcophagus lid with the strange drawings that looked to many like the Mayan monarch was piloting a spacecraft.

Once he had the money and the power to make things happen TNT could afford to indulge his curiosity and his interests. He wanted to know more about the legends of Palenque. First he researched which universities were pursuing archaeological efforts in the state of Chiapas and at Palenque itself. The results of that research yielded only one name – Sussex University in Pennsylvania.

Sussex's archaeological department was on the forefront of exploration in Central and South America. Over the past ten years the school had been granted more licenses to carry out digs in that area than any other institution. Their teams had achieved notable success more than once, making important discoveries that advanced knowledge of the Maya, Aztec and Olmec peoples.

Having found the institution he needed to approach, Torrance went to step two. He used a tactic he normally reserved for his hostile takeovers in the corporate world. He made a call to the major New York law firm that handled millions of dollars a year in legal work for him and requested a background check.

TNT discovered long ago that knowledge was the ultimate power. If he knew things others didn't, he could prevail against an opponent. Before he publicly disclosed his interest in buying a corporation's stock, before the takeover began, Torrance hired his lawyers to gather every piece of information they could unearth about the people he would be up against. He wanted to know secrets. The darker the better. Knowledge was power.

He did things a little differently with the Sussex investigation. He narrowed the scope of the background check to encompass just those people and things that were germane to the university's archaeological work at Palenque. It took only an hour for Torrance to scan news reports and magazine articles and create a list of names. These were the people he wanted to know about

THE STRANGEST THING

— the Sussex-sponsored archaeological teams that were working in the state of Chiapas.

The university's archaeologists had just completed two small projects at Palenque that consisted of opening previously unexcavated buildings. Nothing of importance was found in either but Torrance noted the names of the students who were part of the team. The dig supervisor on both projects was the same graduate student - Cory Spencer.

Ten days after he requested the background check his attorney called. "As you know, sometimes when you order these reports our people find bits and pieces. Other times they don't find anything. Mr. Torrance, this time we hit the jackpot."

The attorney explained that Cory Spencer, the graduate student at Sussex, was actually Paul Emerson of El Paso, Texas. When he was only eleven, the lawyer said, Emerson had savagely murdered his father and then disappeared. For the past fifteen years his whereabouts had been unknown.

The lawyer said that the discovery had been made by fingerprint comparison. The boy's fingerprints were at the crime scene. Years later when Bijan Rarities did a background check on Cory Spencer he had been fingerprinted. Bijan's check had been limited to New York Police Department records. The match linking Cory Spencer to a youthful murderer from El Paso wasn't made. But those same fingerprints, matched this time to a national database, revealed the answer to where Paul Emerson had gone.

"Mr. Torrance, ordinarily we're obligated to notify the authorities . . ."

Torrance cut him off with a polite, "Of course, of course, but it's been a long time and this man was just a boy when it happened. It is critical to a project I'm working on that this information remains confidential. And I appreciate that you'll do that as a personal favor. Thank you so much for everything your firm does for me and my companies."

And that was that. Torrance had a secret on someone who was an archaeologist with Sussex University. And what a secret. This was even better than he could have hoped for.

CHAPTER SEVENTEEN
Tuesday
Twelve days after the disappearance

It took less than an hour for President Harry Harrison to find out that Thomas Newton Torrance and Cory Spencer had been alone with the artifact for nearly thirty minutes. It infuriated him that these two might be destroying clues and evidence that might have given information as to Chapman's whereabouts. But he was powerless to act since they were in Mexico.

Brian Sadler had been sequestered in his office all morning. There were a lot of loose ends to tie up before he could be away in Palenque for three or four days. Since he planned to leave tomorrow there was very little time to get things done. He had instructed his assistant to hold his calls and was irritated when a quiet ring interrupted his work.

There was one call he wanted – from Nicole Farber. Brian had awakened missing her even more than usual. He had called her cellphone early this morning but it went straight to voicemail. He glanced up, saw his private line blinking and touched the speaker button. His heart pounded at the anticipation of hearing her voice.

"Hi, babe."

The same professional female voice he'd heard once before said, "Mr. Sadler, this is the White House. May I transfer a call from the President?"

"Certainly." Brian's disappointment was mixed with a tinge of exhilaration. *I'm on a call with the President of the United States. No other person on earth can make that statement right now. Even if it's old Harry Harrison it still makes you a little tingly.*

After a pause he heard Harry's voice. "Good morning, Brian. Where are you?"

"Good morning, Mr. Pres . . . er, Harry. I'm at the gallery in New York wrapping things up before the trip tomorrow."

"OK. Brian, I just have a minute but I have some news for you. We talked about Thomas Newton Torrance when you were in my office. Turns out he gets around. You know they tried to bring up the artifact yesterday. TNT flew from London and was at the temple in Palenque for the aborted attempt. Then he took your old employee Cory Spencer down into the chamber with

134

him. For some reason Dr. Ortiz, the government's archaeological director, granted Torrance and Cory permission to go alone - without any of the government people along. They were down inside the temple for about thirty minutes.

"Ortiz sent people down the minute those guys got out of the tomb and nothing seemed out of place, at least as far as we've heard. I'd like you to meet up with this Thomas Torrance. Find out what he's up to. There's something going on with him. I want to know what he's doing and if he had anything to do with John Chapman's disappearance."

Harry Harrison promised that the FBI agent at the Palenque airport would hand Brian a briefing file. It would be a current synopsis of everything they knew about Torrance's activities in Chiapas state, his mode of travel and anything else that might be helpful to Brian. It would also contain letters of introduction that might help smooth the way for Brian to get things done. He might not need them but then again they might come in handy.

"The Foreign Secretary of Mexico and our Ambassador know you're coming at my request," the President said. "There was no way to keep your visit quiet — you're flying on a government jet with a flight plan filed to Palenque. But I asked the Ambassador to let you work unhindered unless you request assistance. His contact information will be in the briefing sheet you'll get. Use it if you get in a jam or need something urgently."

After the call ended Brian stared at the phone, thinking. He picked up the receiver and entered a number. He was disappointed as a voice answered, "Miss Farber's office. This is Ryan Coleman. How may I help you?"

"Ryan, this is Brian. Is she around?"

"She is, Mr. Sadler, but she's in one of the conference rooms taking a deposition. I don't expect her back for a couple of hours. May I ask her to call you?"

"Tell her it's nothing urgent but please call me when she has a few minutes. Tell her everything's OK. I just felt like we didn't finish things last night . . ." He immediately regretted having said so much to Nicole's assistant. "Never mind, Ryan. Just ask her to call if she gets a chance sometime."

He looked at the pile of paperwork on his desk awaiting his attention. But all he could think about was Nicole. He felt as though his personal life was falling apart right in front of him. All because of a girl. All because of Nicole damned Farber.

CHAPTER EIGHTEEN
Wednesday
Thirteen days after the disappearance

The same sleek Gulfstream G650 that had transported President John Chapman to Mexico nearly two weeks ago now sat at Teterboro Airport in New Jersey, not far from Manhattan. The plane was fueled, the pilots and crew were standing by, awaiting the arrival of Brian Sadler. He would be delivered to the tiny Palenque airport, just as the President had been. He would be met by a representative of the United States government, just as Chapman had. But Brian's escort to the ruins would be the FBI, not the Ambassador. Brian had awakened several times last night hoping that's where the similarity ended since Chapman's fate was still unknown.

Brian had been picked up at his apartment and now was in another of the government's black Ford sedans, this one equipped with flashing lights and a siren. They moved quickly through traffic down 9th Avenue toward the Lincoln Tunnel. The trip was only fifteen miles but New York driving was measured in time, not in distance. At this time of morning the driver had estimated about half an hour not counting any potential traffic delays.

The entire workday yesterday had passed without a word from Nicole. He had reached for the phone a dozen times, almost calling her number, almost making the first move. But it was her turn. He had left a message and she hadn't responded. His heart ached like he was sixteen again.

At seven p.m. Brian called it a day, packed the stuff he wanted to take on his trip and left the gallery. As he walked to his apartment he had heard a ding on his phone. Excitedly grabbing it he saw a text from Nicole.

"Hey there. Sorry about the crazy day today and not getting to talk to you. Off to a late dinner tonight – no hanky panky, all business! I know you leave tomorrow so I'll call when I can. Love you baby."

Brian hadn't slept much the rest of the night.

I feel like shit, Brian thought as he sat in the back seat of the government sedan rubbing his eyes. He had lain in bed awake, struggling over his relationship with her for hours. He wasn't interested in seeing other women. He just wanted to see a lot more of *her.* Was he wrong for not making that happen? It seemed even when he did make the effort to go to Dallas she was usually so busy she had to almost fit him into her calendar. He felt like he needed an appointment to be with the girl he loved. Why was she so damned good at her job? Why couldn't she live where *he* lived, in New York? Or London? Was he more to blame than she for the sorry state of things? And so it went all night long. When his alarm went off at six a.m. he had groggily forced himself out of bed and into the shower.

Soon the sedan was through the tunnel and on Route 3 heading northeast towards Teterboro Airport while Brian thought about Nicole and idly watched the industrial scenery along the route. He had packed light – he had his iPad, a Kindle and some material from the gallery to work on during the trip. A duffel held some clothes; the President had asked Brian to stay two or three days, long enough to interview everyone at the site. Harrison had also authorized the Gulfstream to take him to Mexico City if Brian thought it necessary to meet with governmental officials there.

Because of the heat in southern Mexico, especially in the rain forest where the ruins of Palenque were situated, Brian had brought his jungle shirts and pants, rain-resistant boots and plenty of insect repellent.

He forced himself to stop thinking about Nicole. This hadn't been the best time to leave the gallery with things so busy but Brian had to admit he was excited about the trip. He missed the ruins and any opportunity to get back, especially flying free on a government Gulfstream, was fine with him.

139

A large sign indicated the exit for Teterboro, one of the nation's largest private airports. The car left the highway and pulled up to a secure chain-link fence with a rolling gate. Most people taking a flight from this airport parked outside a small terminal building and walked through a metal detector, then out to one of the private planes nearby. Not so Brian Sadler - credentials were presented to a guard at the gate and the FBI car was waved through. They drove directly to the gleaming white aircraft and Brian was soon in the air following the same flight plan that had taken President John Chapman to Mexico two weeks earlier.

CHAPTER NINETEEN

Thomas Newton Torrance was finishing breakfast on the terrace of La Casa Hermosa. Dr. Ortiz sat across from him, drinking a latte. He had just told TNT that the President of the United States was sending a personal representative to Palenque. In fact, the plane carrying that emissary would be landing at the local airport shortly. "I'll need to leave in ten minutes or so. I presume the man, Senor Brian Sadler, is going straight to the ruins. I will need to be there to meet him as the official representative of the archaeological expedition."

TNT jerked his head up and looked at the archaeologist, astonished. "Brian Sadler? *He's* the emissary from President Harrison?"

Ortiz noticed Torrance's surprise. "That's what I'm told. The Ambassador said the man is an old friend of the President's. He's also a wealthy antiquities dealer from New York. I presume you know him?"

TNT didn't answer immediately. His face blanched as he thought through the implication of this. It was unbelievable! Could the President possibly know the connection between Sadler and Cory Spencer? Torrance didn't believe in coincidences. Of course the President had to be aware that Spencer previously worked for Brian Sadler. There was no other answer. So for what reason did President Harrison send Sadler here?

This could seriously complicate things.

"Are you all right, Mr. Torrance?" Dr. Ortiz asked, noting the concern on his face.

He quickly regained his composure. "Yes, yes. Sorry. I was just trying to recall where I'd heard Brian Sadler's name. I don't actually think I know him – do you?" As he talked Torrance reached inside his suit coat, pulled out a thick envelope and casually laid it on the table between them. Dr. Ortiz lit a cigarette and ignored the envelope. He enjoyed giving information to Mr. Torrance. The rewards were excellent.

"I've never met Senor Sadler although I have of course heard of him. He is highly respected as a dealer in very rare objects and has a famous gallery in New York City. He also apparently fancies himself an amateur archaeologist. I'm not sure what his credentials are or why the President is sending him. I suppose it's just to gather facts; I am not aware if Senor Sadler has any education in archaeology or detective work. In fact I know of nothing that would particularly qualify him to be involved. But this matter is not in my hands and is really of no concern to me. El Presidente of our country has given the approval for Senor Sadler to make inquiries on behalf of el Presidente Harrison. And I must live with that. You must as well, Mr. Torrance. I for one will welcome him on behalf of my country!"

Torrance looked impassively at Dr. Ortiz. *What an idiot. He's treating this whole thing like it's a social visit. He has no idea the danger we may all be in as a result of this man's imminent arrival.*

"We will all welcome him," the entrepreneur replied cordially, his voice belying his seething anger. *Why must I tolerate these stupid people?*

Torrance continued. "I'll see you in the morning back at the site. I want to talk to Brian Sadler so let me know as soon as you find out what his plans are."

Dr. Ortiz nodded as he nonchalantly picked up the bulky envelope from the table. He stood, shook hands with TNT and left the hotel.

CHAPTER TWENTY

The Gulfstream carrying Brian Sadler landed smoothly at Palenque Airport and the ragtag bunch of children swarmed it again, just as when President Chapman had arrived a fortnight earlier. The same little boy retrieved the same cellphone from his pocket, pressed one button and turned it off. He hoped the gringos would continue to come to Mexico. He was happy making twenty pesos every time someone arrived.

As he finished breakfast at the hotel Thomas Newton Torrance's iPhone dinged and he glanced at it briefly. There was no message but he knew that Brian Sadler had landed in Palenque. As he placed the phone back in his jacket pocket it dinged again. This was a text message from Dr. Ortiz.

Torrance read the text then sat back in his chair, concerned even more. *Interesting. Brian Sadler will be staying at this very hotel. I'm not a bit surprised and actually it makes it easier to keep an eye on him.*

Although La Casa Hermosa was the nicest in the area it was only one of several hotels the U.S. government could have chosen for Brian's stay. TNT ticked off various reasons as to why they might want Sadler at Torrance's hotel. Which they obviously did.

Brian Sadler rode in a Nissan Pathfinder that belonged to the Embassy. The driver introduced himself and showed Brian his FBI badge and identification. "This is for you, sir," he said, handing Brian a thick folder. "I'll take you to your hotel first, then to the ruins. It'll only take about twenty minutes for this first leg."

Brian's phone vibrated – he saw a text from a foreign number he didn't recognize. The message read, "This is the Cultural Affairs office of the United States Embassy in Mexico City. The White House has advised that your hotel arrangements have been changed to allow you to stay in the same hotel as Mr. Torrance." *Interesting. That might be helpful in trying to arrange a meeting with him.*

The file the driver had given him contained around fifty pages of material. There was a report, several photographs, an aerial shot of the Palenque ruin site and copies of several web pages. He glanced at the report, which was basically a briefing document with headers and subcategories. The document covered a variety of subjects including the discovery of the artifact, information about Torrance and the disappearance of the President. *I'll read this tonight,* Brian said to himself. He wanted to go to the ruins as soon as possible so there wasn't time to go over this material now.

Shortly they turned off the highway onto a narrow road leading into the jungle. The driver parked in front of a building that had been constructed to resemble a Mayan temple. A small sign in front read "Hotel La Casa Hermosa". The driver parked and Brian got out to the sound of birds noisily cawing in the high trees surrounding the hotel grounds. It was an idyllic setting. Brian thought how much Nicole would love this place.

The FBI agent spoke briefly in Spanish with the desk clerk who handed him a key card. He said, "Mr. Sadler, if you'd like to drop your bags in your room I'll handle the check-in process." They agreed to meet back in the lobby in twenty minutes.

Brian walked down a path from the reception area. He glanced to the left as he passed the terrace of an outdoor restaurant. At this time of day only one guest lingered over breakfast. He was dressed in a coat and tie, unusual for the jungle, Brian mused as he continued walking. The hotel was in a beautiful setting in the forest; it consisted of eight detached rooms down a short pathway from the main building. He reached his cabana, unpacked his suitcase and walked out onto a small back patio that overlooked the jungle. It had a low fence to keep out the crawling things that might slither in from the forest just a few feet away.

As he paused a moment to take in the scenery something clicked in his mind. *Torrance. That's the guy in the restaurant.* Suddenly his cellphone rang. He glanced at the screen. Nicole. "Hey, sweetie."

"Hey, sweetie yourself! Sorry I missed your call earlier. I was in a deposition. Now we're on a quick break so I thought I'd see if I could catch you. Did you get there OK?"

"Yes, I'm at the hotel in Palenque and we're heading over to the ruins in a few minutes. I wanted to talk to you about last night, Nicole . . ."

"Brian, we need to talk when we both have time. You have stuff to do right now and so do I. Let's talk this evening – I should be at home by seven. Want to give me a call or should I call you?"

"Just call me," Brian responded, disappointed at yet another wait. "I'm sure I'll have less going on tonight than you do. I don't know my schedule for today but I'll try to be available at seven. If I don't answer then I'll call you back when I can."

"Seven on the dot, baby. One thing before I go. Everything's OK, Brian. Don't overanalyze things. I love you and I want to be with you whenever I can, just like you told me the other night that you do too. Don't worry about me. I'll talk to you tonight."

Brian stuck his phone in his pocket, put the briefing folder in a dresser drawer and walked toward the main building. He had to put Nicole out of his mind right now and concentrate on why he was here. He needed to figure out what happened to President Chapman.

The sun's harsh glare made it difficult for Brian's eyes to adjust to the shaded dining area where the man had sat at breakfast. He looked around the terrace – the only person there was a waiter cleaning up the table where the man had been.

Brian was looking so intently at the patio to his left that he failed to see Torrance come around the corner.

"Excuse me, Mr. Sadler!" Torrance stepped quickly to one side, narrowly avoiding a collision.

"Oh, sorry. I was . . ." He looked up, at a loss for words. "Uh, have we . . . have we met?"

"No, but I know you by reputation. My name is Thomas Newton Torrance. Call me Thomas, please. May I call you Brian?"

"Of course. Are you staying here?"

TNT smiled broadly. "Please, Brian. I'm certain the United States government, as good as they are at gathering information, has already told you I was here. But I'm more interested in you – what in the world brings you to Chiapas state? Which of the Palenque mysteries are you here to investigate?"

THE STRANGEST THING

The FBI agent strode briskly down the path toward the men, glancing at his watch. He was obviously coming to check on Brian's whereabouts. He saw them talking, then stopped.

"I'll only be a moment," Brian said to him. The agent turned and went back to the lobby.

"Is that your keeper?" Torrance smiled. "We all have one at times, I'm afraid. Right now I suppose mine is Dr. Ortiz from the National Institute. Have you met him?"

"I haven't. Maybe you can introduce us later. I'm sorry, Thomas, but I have to go. I'm on a fairly tight schedule this afternoon. If things work out we could meet up for a drink later this evening."

"That would be good. I'll be happy to share with you what I know about the Palenque expedition so far. Unfortunately I don't think it'll be of any help in finding President Chapman, which I presume is what you're here for."

Brian avoided the statement. "See you later this evening," he responded, shaking hands with Torrance. He turned, walked to the lobby and met the FBI agent.

CHAPTER TWENTY-ONE
Thursday
The day of the disappearance

President John Chapman descended the stone staircase inside the Temple of the Inscriptions. One of the Secret Service agents had set his watch to mark the fifteen minutes alone that the boss had demanded. If he didn't return on time they would come after him.

At the bottom of the stairs the President stepped into King Pakal's tomb chamber. He had visited this place twice before but this time it was different. He glanced at the heavily covered sarcophagus then skirted around it to the newly opened hole in the floor. A ladder was sticking out. As eager as a schoolboy, Chapman climbed down into the chamber below and flipped on the flashlight Dr. Ortiz had given him.

THE STRANGEST THING

"What the hell?" he said out loud as he looked at the metallic object lying on a stone altar in front of him. "What is this thing?" Chapman thought it looked like a piece of a very large model airplane.

As he reached out his hand to touch the artifact a voice behind him said, "Mr. President, I really wouldn't do that if I were you."

CHAPTER TWENTY-TWO
Wednesday
Thirteen days after the disappearance

The government SUV pulled into the parking area at the Palenque ruins. Brian Sadler saw a rotund man in jungle attire and a pith helmet, sweating profusely as he approached the vehicle.

"Buenas tardes, buenas tardes, Senor Sadler! I am Dr. Armando Ortiz," the man said enthusiastically as Brian got out of the back seat with his backpack. "On behalf of the government of Mexico may I welcome you to my site here at Palenque!"

Brian shook Ortiz's hand and thanked him for his personal involvement in Brian's visit. "I know how busy you must be and I appreciate your coming here today."

"Oh yes, I am a very busy man but I am also at your service, Senor Sadler, for the time you are here. And how long will that be?" he asked casually.

"I'm not certain, Dr. Ortiz. It may be several days, depending on how things turn out."

"I was wondering, Senor Sadler, what you would be most interested in seeing while you are at the site? Those of us here are not certain of the purpose of your visit."

Brian chose his words carefully. "It's just a fact-finding mission, you might say. President Harrison asked me to be an extra set of eyes and ears for him. I know everything possible has been done to solve the mystery of President Chapman's disappearance. I'm sure I'll just be confirming what your government and ours already know, which unfortunately isn't much." He smiled at Ortiz. "Is the Sussex University dig supervisor here?"

Ortiz looked surprised. "Cory Spencer? No, Senor Sadler. Do you wish to interview him? I think he is at the barracks where the team is living here at Palenque. Shall I call him to come over?"

"Please."

The three of them, Ortiz, Sadler and the FBI agent, walked on the trail through tall trees toward the Temple of the Inscriptions as Ortiz texted on his phone. "Senor Spencer will be at the temple shortly," he reported to the group.

Standing in the plaza between the Palace and the Temple, Brian Sadler stopped for a moment to take in the beautiful setting. He loved this place. He had last been here a few years back and was captivated by the tranquility of this majestic city. High trees cast shadows on the ancient buildings built long ago by a mysterious civilization that had somehow mastered complex architecture eerily similar to the Egyptians on the other side of the world. The Mayans had placed hundred-ton stones eighty feet in the air atop a massive temple complex. How had these simple people, living in a primitive jungle environment, accomplished it? Who taught them how to create massive buildings that would require heavy machinery if they were erected today?

Every time Brian saw the incredible edifices these people had built the same questions came into his mind. And every time he wondered what the answers really were. Hundreds of books had been written postulating every theory imaginable. On the surface some were incredibly farfetched but then again, were they really? Brian had often thought about the ancient alien theory — the idea that an advanced extraterrestrial civilization brought science, architecture, construction techniques and much more to primitive societies around the world. Was that really crazier than the conclusion "normal" people believed? Did these Indians, living in hundreds of square miles of forest a thousand years ago, just somehow build these massive cities all over the place? Buildings that stretch to the heavens today, all built with hand tools? Hundred-ton stones carved and laid so perfectly in a wall eighty feet above the ground that you can't put a piece of paper in the seams between them?

Lost in reverie, he jumped when he heard, "Brian! Wow! Good to see you!"

Cory Spencer ran toward Brian and hugged him. "I haven't seen you in a couple of years! What are you doing here?"

Dr. Ortiz moved closer, surprised at the friendship these two men obviously shared. He watched them intently.

"It's OK." Brian slapped Cory on the shoulder. "I'm from the government and I'm here to help you!" They both laughed.

"*You're* the emissary from President Harrison? I, uh, I thought maybe he would send someone with . . ."

Brian interrupted, grinning. "You dare to doubt my credentials as an archaeologist and a sleuth? I don't blame you. Don't ask me why the President chose me to come down. But he asked and I accepted and here I am. So I'll do my best. Listen, I want to catch up with you but we can't keep Dr. Ortiz waiting while we rehash your wonderful days at Bijan Rarities. Let's meet for breakfast in the morning. Say eight a.m.? Dr. Ortiz, am I free at eight tomorrow?"

"Whatever you wish, Senor Sadler," the archaeologist said more tersely than he intended.

Covering himself, he smiled. "Your schedule is in your hands. I am merely your facilitator." He watched and listened as the men chatted.

"Great. Then I'll see you at eight, Cory. I'm at La Casa Hermosa."

Cory's concern showed in his eyes for a second. "You are? Uh, I think our backer Thomas Newton Torrance is staying there too. Do you know him?"

"We met less than an hour ago. I'll be seeing him later this evening."

Spencer's entire demeanor changed. He was no longer the jovial guy he had been and a cloud came over his face. He was suddenly serious and his voice broke slightly. "OK, Brian. I'm glad you're here. Really glad. I . . . I need to talk to you and . . . you know, catch up like you said." He stammered as though he had said too much.

Dr. Ortiz watched him closely then took Brian's arm and steered him to the base of the Temple of the Inscriptions.

Ortiz turned to Spencer and dismissively said, "Cory, I won't need you for this part so you're free to leave now. Senor Sadler, shall we climb the edifice?"

Cory walked back to the team's barracks. Who would have imagined Brian Sadler would drop into his life? *And now, finally, I have a way out of this mess.*

CHAPTER TWENTY-THREE

Cory Spencer's cellphone rang less than twenty minutes after he left Brian Sadler. A pang of anxiety shot through his mind as he saw Thomas Newton Torrance's number on the screen. He had to be careful. Very careful. But he was confident too. Now he had a plan - he knew how he was going to handle all of this.

"Hi, Mr. Torrance."

The financier's voice was steely. "Cory, I hear you met an old friend."

Word gets around fast. "Yes sir, I did. My old boss, Brian Sadler. But I hear you already met him yourself. And I'm sure you know we used to work together. Did Dr. Ortiz call you about my meeting Brian?"

"I know everything about you, Cory. For instance, I know you're going to keep secrets to yourself

157

when you have your little meeting with Sadler tomorrow morning. Aren't you? It would be very dangerous for you and your career if you accidentally, or even on purpose, told things that I don't want you to tell."

Cory was cautious. "We're just having a casual breakfast, sir. We're just catching up on old times."

"Of course you are. I'll be listening. You can count on that. Watching too. I want you to find out something tomorrow. Find out why Brian Sadler is here, why the President picked *him* to come to the temple. Don't arouse his suspicions or cause him to question your interest.

"Cory, you're far, far out of your league here. You have such a minor role it's hardly worth mentioning. But you're going to help me. Why? Because you'll find yourself with a bigger problem than you ever imagined possible if you tell what's happening here at Palenque. You hold your future, perhaps your life, in your hands." Torrance hung up.

Cory shook uncontrollably as he stared at the phone. As quickly as he had worked out a solution he felt mired in his problems again. Torrance was dangerous. Cory had already figured that out. He didn't get where he is by being Mr. Friendly.

My life is in my hands? And he'll be watching and listening? Does he already know about the cavern at the end of the passageway? Is that what he's talking about? Is that what he wants me to keep secret?

158

THE STRANGEST THING

He dropped the phone on his bunk as tears began to flow. *What the hell is going on here? What have I gotten myself into? Who can I trust? Should I trust Brian? If I don't, how can I ever get out of this?*

At 5:30 Brian, Dr. Ortiz and the FBI agent left the chambers, climbed the staircase inside the Temple of the Inscriptions and emerged in the stone building high atop the edifice. They had spent nearly three hours in the two rooms deep inside the temple and the sun was almost down. Dr. Ortiz passed out headlamps from his backpack and the three men walked down the outside of the temple to the broad plaza below. In the growing darkness they walked down the jungle path to the parking lot where the SUV sat.

Brian had offered to let the agent have the afternoon off but he respectfully declined. "Given that President Chapman disappeared from this very place, Mr. Sadler, I don't think President Harrison would take too kindly if I let you out of my sight." The agent had helped them scour the walls, ceilings and floors of King Pakal's tomb and the new chamber below it, the one containing the metal artifact. They had no idea what they were looking for, if anything. All they knew was the President couldn't have vanished from the face of the earth. He had to have gone somewhere, and it wasn't back up the stairway. So there must be something here that they couldn't see.

Brian's excitement was at its peak when they descended for the first time and entered Pakal's burial chamber. His anticipation at seeing the mysterious sarcophagus lid depicting Pakal in what looked like a spaceship was as high this time as when he had first laid eyes on it several years ago. He was disappointed when he saw the lid covered in protective layers of foam and cloth. Then his enthusiasm peaked again – before him lay the hole in the floor leading to the hidden room below.

He was absolutely stunned when he saw the metal strut lying on its stone altar in the chamber below Pakal's sarcophagus. He stood transfixed as he thought about how King Pakal himself must have ordered the construction of his tomb right on top of this artifact that looked as though it were created only a couple of years ago, then involved in a major wreck. What was it? How did it get here? Did it have something to do with Pakal's tomb lid – was this the reason the king ordered his people to depict him lying prone with his hands on levers, preparing to ascend in some type of craft? Was this piece of metal actually a strut from that ship? That thought was too vast, too difficult to comprehend. If it was a strut the entire realm of knowledge of the Mayan people was subject to rethinking. Dramatically. Maybe these weren't just simple natives with no tools. The Spanish conquistadors had burned literally all but five of the Mayan people's written records. Maybe some of those lost books – the codices – had contained records of the Mayan people and their contact with . . . whatever. It was just mind-boggling.

THE STRANGEST THING

After shooting a dozen pictures from every angle with his phone Brian had forced himself to stop staring at the metal strut and join the others to search for another way out of either room. They hadn't found anything today. Hopefully tomorrow would be different.

The men were standing by the government SUV when Dr. Ortiz's cellphone dinged. He took it out, looked at the screen and said to Brian, "Mr. Torrance is at the hotel and would like to have a drink with you, Senor Sadler. Assuming that is good, he asks when you will return."

"That's fine," Brian responded, remembering his promise to talk to Nicole. "I have a conference call at seven so maybe we could meet shortly. If we're leaving now, I could be on the patio at six."

Ortiz sent a response. "All right then, I will see you men tomorrow. Is nine a.m. satisfactory, Senor Sadler? If so I will see you right here."

Brian confirmed the time then Ortiz walked to his own vehicle, an old Willys Jeep. He started it, screeched gears noisily and drove off.

A half-hour later Brian and Thomas Newton Torrance sat on the patio of the hotel. There was only one other table occupied - they appeared to be tourists — a man, woman and two children, all speaking German.

They both ordered vodka with tonic and settled back in their chairs. Torrance began the conversation lightly. "I hope you had a productive afternoon, Brian."

"Seeing the artifact was one of the most amazing things of my life. My mind's racing about what it could be. But really nothing else came of our efforts today."

"What exactly are you looking for?"

Brian was cautious. He wanted to know more about Torrance and his reasons for financing this project without divulging much himself. And that wasn't hard because Brian didn't know much at all; neither did the President.

"I really don't know where to start. President Harrison is willing to commit any resource to finding President Chapman, but it's hard to do that when no one has a clue where he is. Or if he's even alive. He disappeared two weeks ago tomorrow. Could he be trapped somewhere? Maybe. We have to hold out hope. What ideas do you have, Thomas?"

The two men had a largely superficial conversation about the missing President. Torrance advised he had nothing of value to contribute to Brian's efforts so the conversation moved to the site itself. They discussed the discovery of the artifact and its chamber and Torrance's interest in archaeology in general. Brian would learn nothing from this conversation except that the man knew a lot more than he was saying. There had to be another, more productive discussion. Brian had to figure out how.

Brian glanced at his watch. It was 6:45 p.m. He excused himself, saying he had to be on a call shortly.

"Say hello to President Harrison," Torrance laughed. Brian didn't respond – the call was no one's business, certainly not the affair of this man he had just met.

CHAPTER TWENTY-FOUR

At 7:30 Brian laid on the bed in his room, glancing frequently at his phone to be sure he hadn't somehow missed her. For the third time, or maybe the fourth, he checked the mute button to confirm the phone would ring when Nicole finally called. He tested the ring tone to be sure something wasn't wrong with it. Seven on the dot, she had said. That was thirty minutes ago. Brian was hungry but didn't want to walk up to the dining room until he spoke with her. He grabbed a Corona – his third of the evening - from a fridge in the bathroom. Dusk had settled into the jungle and the animal noises began in earnest. Brian opened the French doors wide, allowing a breeze and the night sounds in from the patio. When he was out in the wild he loved this time of day. He found the cacophony interesting, soothing. He lay back on his bed and sipped the cool beer.

THE STRANGEST THING

Ten minutes later he was about to give up and go eat. His phone rang. He jumped when he heard the sound he'd been waiting for and tried to keep his voice from sounding anticipatory. He counted to five before he answered, hoping to keep Nicole from knowing how much he'd been waiting for her call.

"Hi there."

"Hi, baby. Sorry I'm late. I guess I say that all the time, don't I? Hope I didn't keep you waiting too long."

"No problem." Brian sounded as casual as he could. "I didn't even notice what time it was. Where have you . . . oh, never mind. Busy day?"

"Yeah, another crazy one. After work I had to meet a guy who wants to buy my Mercedes. That took longer than I thought."

She's selling her convertible? Brian wanted to ask why but didn't. Conversations with Nicole felt strange to him lately. He wanted to scream out the questions. Who is this guy? How'd you know he wanted to buy your car? Where did you meet him? Did you all have a drink? All those questions that jealous boyfriends want to ask their beautiful sexy corporate lawyer millionaire girlfriends when they're sitting in a jungle and she's in Dallas, Texas "meeting a guy." But he held himself in check. He would give every ounce of effort to appear nonchalant. Nonchalant like Nicole appeared to be lately. Not like before.

"So Brian, I have a proposition for you. You're in Palenque. I looked that up on a map and you're not that far from Cancun. I'll clear my calendar for three days the end of this week and meet you there when you're done with your trip. You can have the President's plane drop you there then fly back with me to Dallas and on to New York."

"Cancun?" You could hear the disappointment in his voice. "Why Cancun? I thought both of us said we'd never go there again. I thought we agreed we hated that place. It's too touristy, too 'all inclusive', too college-student spring break, too tacky for us. We always go for upscale."

"Hey, hey. Slow down a sec and give me a chance to show you something. I bet I can change your mind about Cancun. Got your iPad handy?"

Brian retrieved it from the desk across the room and came back to the bed. "Ready," he said.

"Google Manana Beach Resort on the Riviera Maya."

Brian did, and up popped a website showing a beautiful hotel with luxurious accommodations, white sand beaches, pools and intimate restaurants and bars, some nestled by the ocean.

"It looks good," he admitted, thinking they all look good on their websites. "Where did you find it?"

"I researched it. For us. Click on 'gallery' and let me know what you think about the pictures."

As Brian looked, he saw what made Manana Beach different. None of the guests in the photo gallery had a stitch of clothing on. Every person was naked, everywhere at the resort. In the bars, the restaurant, the pool, even playing volleyball with other guests.

"It's clothing optional?"

"Nope, Brian. Better than that. It's 'no clothing allowed.' You aren't just nude. You're nude everywhere, every minute. It's the rule!"

This is more like it! "No shit! And you'd go to a place like that? Where everybody could see every square inch of you?"

"Damn right I would. You know me. I'm usually up for about anything. I did some in-depth checking on this place. They're very discreet, have an excellent reputation and have never had an incident. I think it sounds like a fun few days together. And your point about everybody seeing me au naturel – well, I guess I could have a little fun seeing every square inch of *them* too! And so could you! We'd have to watch out around those twenty-something girls. You might have to stay in the pool all day!"

As she talked, Brian felt himself growing as he thought about Nicole's beautiful naked body. Her perfect breasts, her neatly trimmed hair, her long legs stretching all the way up to . . . and she continued talking.

"We could really get a suntan at Manana Beach, seems to me. And you could probably get other things you want, like, coffee, tea or . . . me." She laughed throatily. He could tell this was turning her on too.

"Damn, Nicole. I'm going to have to take a cold shower after talking to you. I have to give Harry an update tomorrow on the progress, or lack thereof, unfortunately. I'll find out when he wants me to wrap up here. I'll call you and let's book it. There are parts of you I'd see at a nude resort that I haven't seen in awhile. And I've missed. In fact, there's one part of me that misses you a lot right this very minute."

She laughed again. "Me too, Brian. In fact I just had to take off my shorts I'm getting so hot. I don't know how much time you have right now but how about a little phone sex? If you're in, let's get naked and do it!"

And so they did. They'd never done this before. It wasn't the same as being there but it was satisfying in another way. Brian lay back on top of the sheets, his manhood in his hand, phone cradled to his ear as they exchanged words and thoughts and fantasies. He dreamily listened as she graphically described what she was doing to herself at exactly the same time he was here in this room, similarly engaged. His eyes opened lazily as he stroked . . .

THE STRANGEST THING

He let out a yell and jumped off the bed, searching for something to cover himself with. The phone hit the floor with a thud. On the patio where Brian had left the doors wide open, someone was standing in the shadows.

"Brian! Er, sorry Brian!" Cory Spencer was in the patio doorway, his eyes darting around the room, unsuccessfully trying to ignore Brian's nakedness and what he had obviously been up to. Brian grabbed his shorts and pulled them on.

"One sec, Cory," he muttered as he retrieved his phone from the floor. He put it to his ear and heard Nicole yelling.

"Brian. Brian, answer me! Are you hurt?"

"Hey babe. Sorry about that. Someone just came in my room . . ."

Her concern turned to anger. "Someone *came in your room?* While you were doing what you were doing? Who the hell's there, Brian. Who is she?"

"Nicole, calm down." He looked at Cory and said, "Could you give me a minute?" Instead of walking back out on the patio the archaeologist went to Brian's bathroom, closed the door and turned on the water in the shower so he wouldn't hear Brian's conversation. He didn't turn on the light. *That's strange,* Brian thought.

169

"Nicole, Cory Spencer's here, the guy who used to work for Bijan. He's the university's head archaeologist on this dig and I guess he wants to talk to me about something confidential. I had no idea he was coming and he must have scaled the railing on my patio. I had my doors propped open for the breeze - I glanced up and saw him standing there – it startled me and I dropped the phone."

"Well I hope you're as frustrated as I am. I'm lying here stark naked with a buzzing vibrator and a half-finished mission. You go talk to Cory and I'll see if I can get back to where I left off." Her voice softened and he could almost see the smile as she said, "Hey. Maybe it's better to save up for that nude resort we're going to. So maybe I'll quit for tonight! But probably not! Talk to you later, sweetie. I love you." She disconnected.

Brian struggled for a second to come up with a reason why he was masturbating naked while on a phone call but then decided Cory had been the intruder here. It was Cory who had the explaining to do.

He opened the bathroom door. Cory was sitting on the toilet seat in the dark. "What are you doing here?" Brian shut off the shower jet. "And hey. Sorry about that. A little thing my girlfriend and I do when I'm away. You know . . ."

Cory walked around Brian's room turning off all the lights. He shut the French doors and pulled the drapes closed tightly. In the dark he sat in a chair, held his head in his hands and quietly spoke. "We have to talk. I'm in deep trouble and I need your help. I'm in real danger, Brian. Once I tell you what I know you may be in danger too. But I'm afraid of what may happen and I have to let someone else know.

"You *have* to agree to help me, Brian. And you have to promise me you'll help even before I tell you what I know. This is crazy stuff. This is unbelievable stuff. I'll show you what President Harrison sent you here to find. I've also found the answer to theories people have questioned for thousands of years. The way the Egyptians and the Mayans built their huge buildings. How they knew all the complicated science and mathematics they knew. I've found the strangest thing you will ever see in your life."

"Cory, calm down. Of course I'll help you if I can. Are you in trouble? Have you done something wrong? Something illegal? I have to know more before I can figure out how to help. And Cory, all that you just said about how the Mayans and Egyptians built pyramids – that's all great. But you also said you'd show me what the President sent me here to find. What do you mean by that? What do you think he sent me here to find?"

"Here's the deal, Brian. Yeah, I've done something illegal. Yeah, I'm in big trouble. But you have to help me. You *will* help me. I know you will because I can tell you where President Chapman is. *That's* what you're here to find. There's one thing you have to promise me. I have to be involved in the decision when to tell President Harrison what happened here. I won't make you wait long but you and I have to have a plan before you involve the government. I've got to make sure I'm covered here."

"I can't do that. I can't make a promise like that. You don't know what you're asking . . ."

"I *do* know what I'm asking, Brian. Nobody has ever dealt with this before. Either part of this. No one has ever seen what I found. And nobody has ever dealt with a missing President. Just work out a plan with me. If you promise me that, I'll tell you everything. If you can't promise that I'll leave and figure things out alone. But you can't renege if you make that promise. My life hangs in the balance here. Literally."

"It's a deal," Brian said at last, "but forty-eight hours is all you get."

CHAPTER TWENTY-FIVE

Cory Spencer told Brian everything that happened on the day President John Chapman disappeared. Brian listened to the entire story without saying a word.

"Mr. President, I really wouldn't do that if I were you."

Startled, President John Chapman jerked his hand back from the metal artifact lying in front of him. He thought he was by himself in the chamber, his agents waiting for him at the top of the temple. He thought he had fifteen minutes to look at this amazing discovery alone.

Chapman's immediate reaction was anger, not fear. "Who the hell are you and how'd you get in here?"

"There's a passageway, Mr. President. I came out of it. There's a hidden passage and you need to see what's beyond it. I'm Cory Spencer, sir." He held out his hand to shake the President's. "I'm the lead archaeologist from Sussex University."

John Chapman visibly relaxed once he heard the name. He now recalled seeing Spencer's picture in an archaeology magazine and knew he was telling the truth about who he was. "You surprised the hell out of me," he snapped. "What are you doing here?"

"I'm sorry, Mr. President. I figured I might startle you but I'd never have been able to get in here with you if I'd done things the proper way. You need to see this. And sir, don't touch the artifact. It's highly radioactive."

"I want to know why you decided to show this to me. The problem is, I only have about ten minutes before the storm troopers come crashing down that stairway. Let's see what you've found that's so important then we'll talk back upstairs."

"I'll tell you everything, sir, once I show you what I've found."

Cory walked to the far end of the room, stood between the stone altar and the wall. He extended his arms sideways. His fingers searched and found what he wanted.

THE STRANGEST THING

"I'll be damned." The President watched as a large stone moved silently back into the darkness, revealing a passageway beyond. "How'd you figure that out?"

"No time now, sir." The archaeologist flipped on his flashlight and led the way. Once they were inside the corridor he pressed an almost-invisible indentation on the wall and the stone swung shut behind them.

"Hang on a second," President Chapman shouted, alarmed. "Open that back up right now . . ."

"Mr. President, I'm willing to show you something so incredible you absolutely won't believe it. But you have to let me do it my way. I'm not ready to let anyone else know about this. You're completely safe but I'm not going to leave it open. I promise you it'll open back up when we're done."

The President wasn't accustomed to people ignoring his demands. "OK, Cory. This better be good or you're in a deep pile of shit, buddy. You know that?"

Cory ignored the question and led John Chapman down the corridor several feet. His flashlight cast ghostly shadows on the walls and floor. As the men moved past two glyphs carved into the hallway Cory pointed them out to the President. "What are they?" he said, taking time to briefly stare at each one.

"The first one'll become obvious in a moment, sir. The other one will too once you think about what

I'm going to show you. We don't have time to look at these closely, Mr. President. I just want you to see what's in the cavern ahead of us."

The passageway ended and they stepped into an enormous room a hundred feet or more long, its ceiling towering above them. Thirty feet in front of them, roughly in the middle of the room, there was some debris. Cory shined the light on it. "Right here, sir."

There were two mangled pieces of metal lying on the ground. They were like the two oval pieces of a plastic Easter egg – at one time they undoubtedly had fit together but now they were lying side by side as though they had been wrenched apart in an accident.

The pieces were roughly twenty feet long and eight feet wide. One, obviously the top, had rows of a glasslike material that appeared to be windows. As Cory held the light the President looked at it then turned his gaze upon the other section.

The other oval object, the bottom part, was more heavily damaged. On its undersurface were three struts. A fourth was missing, ripped off in what appeared to have been a disastrous calamity of some sort. All four would have kept the object upright; with only three it lay tilted.

"That thing, that metal strut back there in the chamber you discovered, it belongs right here, doesn't it?"

"Yes sir, it does. It's identical to the other three that are still attached."

Chapman peered closely at the interior of the oval object.

"What are those . . . oh dear God. Are those . . . This looks just like the glyph back there . . ."

"You're absolutely right, sir. Those small white capsules are the same things depicted on the first glyph back in the passageway. There are fifteen of them – I counted them. I think . . . well sir, just between you and me I think they're some sort of beings. I know that sounds crazy . . ."

The President was stunned. He didn't move for several seconds. When he spoke his voice was a whisper. "Yeah, Cory, I have to agree with you. I think those things were in this craft when it crashed. It may be crazy but I can't think of anything better."

Chapman looked at the archaeologist, thinking out loud. "Who drew the glyphs on the corridor wall? They don't look Mayan."

"No way to tell for sure, Mr. President, but I figure somehow these things did. And look at this." Cory pointed to the outside of the "lid" of the oval metal egg. Etched into the metal was an exact duplicate of the second glyph – a lot of circles in various positions around two large ones.

"Do you think . . . Cory, is it possible this depicts the place they came from? Do these circles represent planets revolving around . . ."

Suddenly Chapman stepped backwards. "Shit!" he yelled, raising his left leg into the air.

Cory turned the light on the President. Through his left pant leg a four-foot snake had embedded its fangs into Chapman's thigh. The archaeologist recognized it immediately – a fer-de-lance. Aggressive and almost always lethal. Chapman had obviously disturbed it - probably he had stepped on it - and the snake had attacked.

The President of the United States of America fell to the ground next to Cory Spencer. The archaeologist panicked. He withdrew a knife from his pocket and stabbed the snake in its head, careful to stay clear of its mouth when the viper released its hold. Once he made sure the snake was dead Cory shook the President's body, pumped his chest and attempted to give him CPR. He knew from experience that these attempts were useless but he had to try.

Once before Cory had seen a fer-de-lance strike a human. It was at an archaeological site in Guatemala and one of the workmen had been bitten after sticking his hand under a rock in a cave. He had died almost instantly. Having seen that, Cory knew there was absolutely nothing he could do for Chapman but he worked for ten fruitless minutes. It was over - the

THE STRANGEST THING

President had died less than sixty seconds after he was bitten.

Cory stopped and sat on the ground next to Chapman's body. He shook uncontrollably and tears flowed. "Shit. What am I going to do about this? What will they think about why I took the President in here? How much trouble will this be for me? I just made the most amazing discovery in the history of the earth and now It's all going down the drain." *Think. Think, man. You have to* think. *Figure something out.*

CHAPTER TWENTY-SIX

"Brian, I just didn't know what to do. I still don't. Until you got here I didn't think I had a chance even to live. I'm scared to death of Thomas Newton Torrance. I absolutely believe he's going to kill me after he gets what he wants and I show him what I've found."

"Who else knows about this, Cory? You know this thing can't be kept secret."

"Mr. Torrance knows I found a passageway and about the glyphs. He doesn't know about the craft or the white capsules. I also told him I found the President's body – he doesn't know I was there when it happened. As soon as I found out they were going to televise the raising of the artifact I notified TNT – I owed him that as our backer. When they got into the chamber and began working to hoist up the artifact I figured there was a big chance that someone else might discover the passageway.

THE STRANGEST THING

I decided to tell him about the glyphs and the President but I didn't give him any information as to how it happened. I made it sound like I never walked to the end of the passageway. He thinks the President's body is right at the front of the passage and he has no idea there's some kind of craft in the cavern."

"And he hasn't asked to see it?"

"Oh sure he has, but there hasn't been a chance. We went down to the chamber and talked on the day they tried to raise the artifact but he was unwilling to have me open the passage with people nearby. He's pushing now for a time to see it. I'll have to get in there at night. That's the only way. Brian, can you help me? I thought everything would be OK here. I had a great plan to "rediscover" the passageway and find the President dead from a snakebite. But I made a mistake telling Mr. Torrance. I think he'll do anything to get this for himself. He won't let anyone stand in his way. I think he'd kill me, Brian. I really do."

"OK. Let me ask you a few more questions. What did you do after the President died?"

"I completely went to pieces, like I told you. I sat there maybe an hour, maybe more. I tried to think what to do but I couldn't come up with anything. So I went back to the front of the passageway to go out and heard faint voices, shouts, through the stone wall. I suddenly realized what had to be going on. The President had said he only had about ten minutes in the chamber alone. His security people must have come looking for him. And they wouldn't leave. They'd be there all day, maybe even all night, trying to find him. I hoped they wouldn't find the way in, but in the meantime *I couldn't leave.*"

"How'd you finally get out?"

"I waited all day. I kept turning my flashlight off to conserve batteries. At around nine o'clock I couldn't hear any sounds through the wall so I made the decision to open the passageway door. If I had gotten caught then it would be all over. But I didn't. The chamber and Pakal's tomb were empty. I climbed the stairway and unlocked the gate from the inside. I quietly raised it up, locked it back and looked outside. I saw some people down below me in the plaza. They were guards - one was smoking a cigarette and I saw its glow. So I sneaked down the side of the pyramid. It was tough but I kept quiet, made it down and back to the barracks."

"What happened then?"

"First thing I did when I got back was to look at my phone. Mr. Torrance had called maybe ten times and texted at least that many. He got more and more insistent in his voicemails and texts that I get in touch with him."

Cory showed Brian some of the texts. *Insistent isn't exactly the right word for these,* Brian thought. They were demanding, threatening.

"Cory, you need to leave this with me for now. I need to think about this and we'll figure out a solution. If everything happened the way you say, there's nothing to be afraid of. I promise you I won't desert you or let you get into trouble over this. The President has enormous power. You just have to let me take charge of this for now. OK?"

"OK, Brian."

"Meet me tomorrow at 8 a.m. at the temple. I'll talk to Dr. Ortiz and get permission for us to go in there by ourselves."

"Thanks. Like I said if you hadn't come I don't know what I would have done. Now at least I have hope."

They exchanged cellphone numbers to keep in touch. The archaeologist left Brian's room through the patio door, just as he had entered. They had talked for over an hour.

Sitting in his cabana less than five hundred feet from Brian's, Thomas Newton Torrance removed the headset once he heard the two men finish their conversation.

He waited three hours. Around midnight he made a phone call.

CHAPTER TWENTY-SEVEN
Thursday
Two weeks after the disappearance

A little after midnight two men were making their ways through the jungle. The shrieks of howler monkeys high in the trees above them were shrill and unearthly. The dense forest was alive with sound, a choir of animal voices coming from all directions.

Thomas Newton Torrance was more accustomed to limousines in London than trekking through the Mexican undergrowth in the middle of the night but this was a critical trip. Now that he knew exactly what Cory Spencer had found he had to see it himself, deal with Cory and implement the plan he had developed. Since Brian Sadler knew about it too, time was quickly running out. Cory's clandestine meeting with Sadler earlier this evening had changed everything.

THE STRANGEST THING

Immediately following the aborted attempt to bring up the metal artifact, Torrance and Cory Spencer had visited the chamber. That time TNT had resisted seeing what Cory had discovered – it wasn't safe with Dr. Ortiz standing by at the top of the temple. Thomas Newton Torrance had patiently waited for an opportunity to see for himself what Cory Spencer had found – the hidden passageway with an amazing secret.

The fact that President Chapman's body lay in the cavern was a minor issue in the scheme of things. Torrance would deal with that. He had been formulating a plan that would solve everything and give him sole control of the rarest single thing ever discovered on planet Earth. And that wouldn't change now. It just had to be implemented immediately.

After leaving Brian's cabana Cory had walked quietly back to his room in the barracks. Most of the student diggers had been sent back to Sussex University – there was nothing left for them to do. Only a few of the team remained – they were playing cards at a table in the bunkhouse and barely acknowledged his entry. By ten p.m. he had fallen into a light sleep – the restless kind when there's a lot on your mind. After telling Brian everything he had felt much better; at least someone else knew what was going on. Cory felt certain he could delay showing Torrance the secret passageway and cavern now that Brian was helping him. It was all going to work out.

Cory's phone had rung at midnight. "Meet me outside your barracks at 3 a.m. Bring a flashlight and the key," Torrance had said. Then he hung up. Spencer lay in his bunk, suddenly drenched in sweat.

What was going on? Why did Torrance want to see him? Could he know about Cory's meeting tonight with Brian? There was no way; Cory had been extremely careful and knew he hadn't been seen coming or going.

I have to talk to Brian about this. He got dressed, grabbed a light and his keys and stepped outside the bunkhouse to call Brian. Everyone else was asleep. *Good.*

Cory was careful not to let the screen door bang shut behind him. He saw no one but in a few seconds he heard a low voice. "Hello, Cory. You're up a little early for our 3 a.m. meeting, aren't you?" Torrance stood in the trees wearing a headlamp that was turned off.

"What are you doing here? I was just going to check on something . . ."

"Enough, Cory. Enough lies. We're going to see the passage."

"Now? Uh, I don't think . . ."

"No, you *don't* think, Cory. That's the problem. We're going to see the passage. Now. Take us through the jungle. I want to avoid the pathways and the night watchman's station. Do you have the key to unlock the gate?"

THE STRANGEST THING

It was impossible to miss the steely hardness in Torrance's voice. An involuntary shudder of fear engulfed the archaeologist.

"The key's in my pocket."

"Go in front," Torrance said. "Now."

The two men carefully walked through the dense jungle. Cory Spencer stayed ahead of Torrance and used his flashlight. TNT had one too. Spencer heard the noisy screeches and howls but ignored them; he was on guard for things that made no sounds. He scanned trees and ground, watching for one of many jungle dwellers whose poison could paralyze a man in thirty seconds. The snakes could kill a man quickly, as Cory well knew from what had happened to President Chapman. Out here in the jungle there were other silent predators, such as the big cats, that pounced and tore their prey into pieces while it was still alive. The rain forest at night was not a place for men. It belonged to those who lived and died here, sometimes the hunter, sometimes the prey.

"How much further?" TNT quietly asked. It would have taken less than ten minutes if they'd stayed on the cleared pathways from the archaeological barracks to the ruins. By going through the jungle it added at least a half hour and a lot more effort.

"Maybe five minutes," Cory responded, his voice quivering. "Keep your light pointed in front of you and look side to side as we brush through this undergrowth. We don't need anything biting us."

TNT was seriously afraid of snakes although he hadn't revealed that to the people here in Mexico. During the walk through the jungle he had occasionally gotten so far behind Cory that he almost lost sight of him. That was because Torrance was being overly cautious and watching his every step. Each time he realized he was too far back he quickly caught up. It was better to be close behind the guy who was forging the trail, TNT thought. Safety in numbers and all that. He had a fleeting thought that a jaguar could kill them both before either had time to react.

Finally they broke out of the dense undergrowth. Still in the forest, the trees now were spaced far apart and the underbrush had been cleared. TNT relaxed.

"We're in the northeastern sector of the Archaeological Zone now," Cory whispered. Similar to a national park in the States, this was the large area that had been designated a historic preserve. "We don't have far to go."

Cory checked his compass and altered his direction slightly. In a moment they came to the open plaza by the huge structure called The Palace. Behind it was the beautiful Temple of the Inscriptions, almost ghostly in the moonlight.

In the eerie brightness of the moon they scaled the temple without flashlights. Far above the ground they entered the gaping doorway that led to the stone stairway and Pakal's tomb. The iron gate over the top of the stairs was securely padlocked.

The archaeologist fished the key out of his pocket, unlocked the gate and lifted it up. It was fortunate for TNT that Dr. Ortiz had provided the lead archaeologist with a key. TNT would have far preferred being alone tonight. What he now knew he would see was so incredible he wanted it all for himself. But he needed the Cory, especially now that the archaeologist had involved Brian Sadler in the secret of the temple. Cory had sealed his own fate when he made that decision, TNT mused. *But it's of no importance to me. It was his decision so he'll live with the consequences. Or die, actually.* Torrance smiled at the pun.

The two men descended the stairway inside the Temple of the Inscriptions and reached the tomb of King Pakal. They were both using headlamps. The protective covering over the king's tomb had been removed and the drawings on the sarcophagus lid took on a frightening aspect as the light played over them. King Pakal's countenance glared upwards towards the Mayan god sitting atop the mysterious craft Pakal seemed to be riding in.

"Ready to go down?" Cory asked. He was resigned to the fact that tonight Thomas Newton Torrance would learn the truth. And he struggled to think how he would work all this out. This man wouldn't bully him any longer. As soon as he got out he'd tell Brian that Torrance had seen the secret passageway and the cavern. Since TNT now would know what happened

189

to President Chapman, this would change Brian's planning. But Cory had faith that his old boss would figure something out.

Cory started down the ladder and Torrance descended after him. The archaeologist walked to the wall directly behind the stone altar where the metallic artifact lay.

"Here's how it works," he said. "It was purely by chance I noticed this small recess in one stone of the altar under the artifact. I put my hand there to steady myself while I looked at the metal strut, and I felt it. It's like a little depression, so small you'd never see it. I only found it because I *felt* it." He pointed to a round indentation that was impossible to see. It looked exactly like the rest of the rock. In all the searches neither the FBI, the Mexican authorities nor Brian Sadler had located it.

"I stuck my finger in it but nothing happened. I thought about it all night and wondered if there might be a second indentation somewhere close by. The next day I was closing up the site – I had sent everyone else out – and I looked closely at the wall opposite the first button I found."

In the same end of the chamber where Cory had found the first small indentation there was a second depression, this time in the wall. About shoulder high, it blended perfectly with the rock. It was something a person would never have noticed unless he had found the first one and knew to look for another. It was about three feet from the first "button," the one in the altar

190

itself. By sheer luck Cory had stumbled upon both depressions. You could look forever, Torrance thought, and never see either one.

"I worked for fifteen minutes trying to figure out how it might operate. I pressed one, then the other. I had almost given up when I pressed them both at the same time."

Positioning his left hand over the small round indentation under the artifact, he reached his right hand over to the identical depression in the wall. Hands outstretched, he pressed both at the same time. A rock about the size of a refrigerator swung noiselessly backwards into the wall, revealing a dark stone passageway about three feet wide and five to six feet high.

"Will the stone door stay open?" TNT asked.

"I don't know. All I know is that these two buttons will both open and close it. When I found it I immediately closed it back so I could show it to you. I haven't checked it out since because I was afraid I might get trapped inside. This is the first time I've opened it since then." Cory didn't mention the other thing he had discovered – that the massive stone door could be operated from *inside* the passage as well as from the chamber outside.

Torrance walked inside the corridor. Already knowing the answer he said, "Where's the President's body? I thought you said it was right here."

Cory's voice quivered as he spoke. Torrance watched his face then spoke harshly. "You said the President's body was here at the beginning of the corridor. You said there were two glyphs etched into the passageway further down but that you never went to the end of the hallway. Is all of that true? If so, where pray tell is the President's body, Cory?"

"I didn't tell you everything earlier about what's in here."

"Tonight when you told Brian Sadler, was *that* the truth? Was I the only one you lied to?" Torrance pulled a small pistol from his pocket and aimed it at Cory Spencer.

"How . . . er, why do you think I said anything to Brian?" Cory moved to the wall, propping himself up with his arm — he looked as though he were about to faint.

TNT shook his head, smiling.

"I told you I could hear and see everything you were doing. And you, you idiot, didn't believe I had the capability to do that. But I really do, Cory. I heard the entire story — every word you told Brian Sadler this evening."

Torrance had listened to the conversation courtesy of devices he had ordered Dr. Ortiz to install. The audio pods were all over the patio dining area and

THE STRANGEST THING

Brian's room. There was nothing anyone could say in either place that would go unheard.

"Walk ahead of me down the passage," Torrance ordered, waving the gun to indicate he should start moving.

As Cory pushed away from the wall the huge stone door behind him suddenly closed with no sound but a click. He had pressed the button as he leaned against the rocks.

Snakes weren't the only things that made Thomas Newton Torrance afraid. He wasn't too wild about dark narrow enclosures deep beneath the ground either.

"Very clever, Cory. I see you discovered a way to control the door from *inside* the passageway. Now open it."

"Give me the gun and I'll open the door."

"You give me such little credit. Do you truly think you can outsmart me? I'll figure out the door later, with your help or without it. Now walk down the passageway ahead of me." He gestured ahead with the gun and Cory began to walk, shining his flashlight on the wall to his left.

About five feet down the corridor Cory stopped and directed his flashlight beam at the first glyph. Careful to keep an eye on him, Torrance stood in front of the hieroglyph carved into the wall. He marveled at its beauty and gasped as he appreciated what it represented.

It was roughly four feet by two, intricately detailed and beautifully painted – the most astounding glyph he had ever seen. It was here among the Maya, in a temple in fact, but it was dramatically different from those usually associated with this culture. Struggling for a word to describe it, Torrance thought of "modern." Most Maya glyphs were beautiful and intricate but they were clearly drawings made a long time ago by a people who somewhat crudely drew gods, animals and humans.

This glyph was undoubtedly ancient. It had to be – here it sat, carved into the wall of a hidden passageway beneath a fifteen hundred year old tomb. But it looked like a rock drawing of something modern. TNT thought it looked abstract - a lot of little capsules that resembled the pills doctors prescribe, only larger, lying in some kind of oval nest. It was detailed enough that he could make out that each seemed to be wearing some kind of hat with earflaps like you'd wear in cold weather. Four tiny appendanges stuck out from each capsule – the hands and feet, if that's what they were, ended in round circles instead of fingers and toes. Many of them were grouped in threes on top of each other like the circular parts of little snowmen. He counted them – there were fifteen in all. Fifteen little capsules in a large oval bowl. That's exactly what they looked like.

"Go on," he said at last, reluctant to leave this wonder but equally interested in what he knew was ahead.

THE STRANGEST THING

Cory walked a few feet further then shone his light on the second glyph. This one was another abstract drawing of some kind but it was totally different from the nest of capsules in the first glyph. This one showed fifteen circles in various positions around two large ones in the middle. Like the other, this glyph was painted in vivid colors of green, blue and red. The large middle circles were yellow, like the sun.

"You know what this means . . ." Torrance muttered to himself.

"I know what it means, Mr. Torrance. So will you when you see what's in the cavern."

As Cory walked on Torrance saw the tunnel end about ten feet ahead. It was pitch black except for the beam of their lights so it was impossible to see what was coming up. Keeping his head down to avoid bumping the low ceiling he followed the archaeologist as they both stepped out of the passage and into a room.

They stood in the cavern President Chapman had marveled at. Torrance shone his light around - what he saw in the middle of the massive room literally took his breath away. Even after having heard Cory tell Brian Sadler about it Torrance still was astonished. He wasn't totally *surprised;* for thousands of years people had pondered certain mysteries and TNT had long thought what the answer to those questions might be. But he was amazed – lightheaded. He was seeing something so unbelievable it was almost incomprehensible. He never expected it to be like this. And he had never expected to see it himself.

Thomas Newton Torrance walked forward to the pile of metal lying roughly in the center of the cavern. Forgetting about Cory Spencer, TNT stood transfixed in front of the most amazing thing on earth. Or anywhere else, for that matter.

Cory took a step toward him.

Jolted back into reality, Torrance raised his gun hand back up. "Stay where you are."

Satisfied that Spencer couldn't rush him from that distance, Torrance looked back at the egg-shaped metal object. He wanted to touch one of the capsule-like things that lay before him. He counted fifteen - they looked old and dusty, having lain for well over a thousand years locked in this hidden cavern. *Wonder how long they really have been here?* Torrance thought. He reached out his hand over the capsule things but paused. The strut had been radioactive. These could be the same, so touching them was unwise. Reflexively he pulled back his hand quickly and stepped backward.

As he did so Torrance tripped and fell to the ground, his gun skittering one way on the sandy floor as his flashlight rolled another. He had fallen over something – he reached out in the semi-darkness and felt it, realizing he had momentarily forgotten about the body of John Chapman. As he started to get up he saw Cory's

THE STRANGEST THING

light find the gun. The archaeologist quickly picked it up and aimed it at Torrance.

CHAPTER TWENTY-EIGHT

"This is the end of your controlling me, Mr. Torrance. You're not running the show any more. From here on I am. You can't get out unless I show you how. You'll never find the way."

Surprised at Cory's sudden bravado, TNT snapped, "Cory, you'll do what I say. If you don't . . ."

The archaeologist interrupted. "I'm tired of all the things you're going to do if I don't obey you. I've done some bad things in my life – so have you, I bet – and I can't go on wondering when you're going to drop the bomb on my entire existence. But now I'm calling the shots. Here's what I want from you – here's what *you're* going to do. You're going to promise me you'll never reveal my past. You're going to give me full credit for this discovery and you and your money are going to back me as an archaeologist from now on. Take it or leave it. With you or without you this will work for me."

Torrance didn't answer for almost a minute. He stood defiantly looking at Cory. Finally he responded in a quiet steady voice.

"Have you ever heard anyone say that a person knows so little he doesn't even know what he doesn't know?"

"What does that have to do with me . . ."

"It has *everything* to do with you." Torrance smiled grimly. "Can I pick up my flashlight? I want to show you something."

Cory answered affirmatively. TNT retrieved the light and stepped back over to the middle of the cavern where the oval egg lay with fifteen small capsules inside it. Torrance pointed at it.

"This discovery is so important, so crucial that it will literally change *everything* and you have such a miniscule part in the entire thing that it's almost laughable. You have the delusion that finding an alien spacecraft in a Mayan tomb is going to advance your career. But it won't. Even if these things are what you think they are. If the announcement of this discovery refers to these things as extraterrestrials you'll be ridiculed, laughed off the stage at scientific meetings, the butt of every joke at every university in the world. From now on. For the rest of your life. Because you have no way to *prove* that these things are alien.

"Academics don't take lightly to having their worlds turned upside-down, Cory. Far from being an instant success, you're going to be an instant buffoon. I promise you that.

"But none of that matters. This is the single most important discovery in the history of our planet. Disclosed to the world properly, this is proof of the thing so many people have believed – that others came before us - that the Mayans, the Egyptians, people in far-flung regions of the remote corners of our world had guidance in building their cities and advancing their civilizations. I can make this happen, Cory, because I have power, influence, money. I have everything you don't have – you're a graduate student in archaeology. I, on the other hand, can ensure this discovery is given the attention it needs. I can get credible people in the scientific community to agree with me. I can make this happen for both of us, whereas you can't make it happen even just for yourself."

Cory hated Thomas Newton Torrance. He hated the condescending attitude Torrance always took with him, and he hated that even now, when Cory was holding a gun, the man still was belittling him. The worst part was Cory knew TNT was right.

The entrepreneur continued. "Any intelligent person can only conclude that primitive Indian tribes who lived in the jungle didn't put a two hundred thousand pound rock sixty feet in the air on top of a building using nothing but stone hand tools. It's ludicrous to think they could. But these things here in this pod – these things knew how to do it. And for whatever reason, they taught these primitive civilizations all these marvelous things we can only wonder about today. I think they taught them architecture, mathematics, science. This discovery can explain some of the most puzzling enigmas of our lives.

"Think of what we can learn from this thing. These people came from another solar system. That's undoubtedly what the second glyph shows. Fifteen planets around two suns. They drew that to let others know where they came from. What knowledge lies inside this egg? This craft flew through space. What advancements in technology can we make by studying it?

"You wonder why I want this. Because I want it *all*, Cory. I have the ability to buy anyone and anything I want. But this is a challenge – the biggest one in the world. The challenge here is to control something absolutely unique. And I'm going to come out the winner in this challenge. I'm going to own the most incredible thing ever found on Earth. You have the gun, Cory. Sadly, that's all you have. You need me. You can't do this without me. So give me the gun and let's figure out how we're going to make this work."

Thomas Newton Torrance stood next to the egg-shaped metal craft and spoke passionately. Cory couldn't help but be caught up in what he was saying. It made sense. Dammit, it made sense. Hanging his head, he handed over the pistol. Torrance took it but instead of putting it in his pocket, he aimed it at the archaeologist.

"Cory, your involvement here is over. You don't have a future with this discovery. Only I do. I don't need you any more and frankly I'm not putting up with you any more. You can show me how to open the stone door and you can walk out of here alive, or I promise you I'll kill you right now and figure it out myself. You can walk away, leave this site tonight and start a new life as a different person, just like Paul Emerson did a long time ago. But this time you'll have enough money to do it right. Ten million dollars. Wired to your account tomorrow morning. I don't want to have to kill you but I want you out of my life forever. You've given me what I want. You've shown me what you found and now it's mine. Not ours, Cory. Mine. What'll it be?"

Cory's response took Torrance completely by surprise. Instead of retreating he took three steps forward, now standing close enough to touch the entrepreneur. TNT stepped back but could go nowhere – he was up against the side of the egg-shaped pod, his back against it. He involuntary raised his free hand to steady himself, the other still aiming the pistol at Cory.

"You're wrong, Mr. Torrance. I do have a future with this discovery. I've lived under your thumb ever since we started this dig. I've been afraid to do anything to cross you for fear you'll tell about my past. But you know what? I'm done with all this. I'll tell you how to open the door and we can share the glory. You've got all the money and all the power. God knows you've told me that enough times. You can figure out how to explain about the President and I guess we'll both get what we want. I want recognition – a career built on discovery – and if this all turns out to be what you think it is, that's exactly what I'll get. You can own whatever this is. If that floats your boat, go for it. I just want credit for finding it.

"You can kill me, Mr. Torrance, but you'll have a much bigger problem than you have now. Brian Sadler *will* figure out how to open the door. I told him enough that he'd eventually find the way. And you'll be sitting right here with both the President of the United States and me dead on the floor. Like I said, I don't care. Do you want to share the glory or not?"

Torrance raised the gun to chest level and smiled. "I never was that good at sharing."

Cory reached out and grabbed TNT's gun hand, attempting to wrench it sideways. Torrance was stronger than Cory had thought; he maintained the gun roughly aimed at the archaeologist. As they struggled Cory pushed Torrance back. The entrepreneur leaned backwards over the metal half-egg and used his free hand to steady himself. His fingers grazed the tops of several of the small capsules lying inside the oval craft. Cory saw something out of the corner of his eye. He opened his mouth to warn Torrance as a shot rang out.

Cory Spencer sprawled on the sand floor of the cavern, a few feet from the body of President John Chapman.

Thomas Newton Torrance fell backwards into the egg-shaped object. He lay immobile on top of the fifteen small capsule-like objects. As soon as his hand had come into contact with them, each began to emit a tiny spark. Now they were glowing brightly all around his body.

CHAPTER TWENTY-NINE

At 5:30 a.m. Brian got out of bed. He had tossed and turned all night, thinking about the implications of what Cory Spencer had disclosed. He had made a promise to a man who believed his life was in imminent danger. Should he honor that commitment or tell the President what he had learned?

Where should my loyalty lie? Brian thought. Brian considered himself an honorable man, one who could be trusted. And he wanted to uphold the promise he made to a desperate Cory Spencer. He also had to find the secret to opening the passageway. For both reasons, Brian decided to hold off. If the President were dead anyway another few hours wouldn't matter. *I meet Cory at eight. Once I see what's in the cavern I'll decide when to call Harry.*

He texted Dr. Ortiz. *Meet me at the temple at 8 a.m.*

As he lay in bed he called Nicole's cellphone. After three rings he was thinking up a clever voicemail when she answered.

"Good morning, sweetie. How'd your secret conversation with the archaeologist go? Or was it really some sultry jungle girl instead?"

"I could only wish," he laughed. "There are some major developments here as a result of what I learned from him, Nicole. Really big. Enormous. I can't discuss anything now – I hope you understand - but I promise once I talk to Harry and the story breaks you'll see it on the news."

"Wow. Good stuff, I hope."

"I have to confirm this for myself but it appears there's something incredible and a closure we all need. That's really all I can say."

"OK. Well, can I plan our trip to Cancun in three days? I'll pack light . . . since I won't need any clothes. Maybe just a gallon of suntan lotion!"

"I'd say book it. Three days should be enough to finish my part of what's going on here."

"See you soon. One hundred percent of you!" She hung up as he smiled.

THE STRANGEST THING

When Brian went through the packet of information the U.S. Embassy had earlier provided he found ten copies of a letter styled To Whom it May Concern. Written on the Ambassador's letterhead, it was a request for cooperation from anyone to whom Brian presented the missive. It stated that Brian had the full backing and support of the President of the United States in any assistance he required.

He pulled one copy of the letter from the envelope, folded it and stuck it in his pocket. He figured he'd have to pull rank on Dr. Ortiz to get into the temple without him. He texted his "keeper," the FBI agent, to advise he wanted to go to the ruins at Palenque at 7:45.

At seven Brian walked over to the dining area. Thomas Newton Torrance wasn't at breakfast but Dr. Ortiz sat on the patio smoking a cigarette and drinking a latte. Brian hadn't expected to see him this early.

"Senor Sadler, come join me." He patted the armchair next to him. "I saw your text a few minutes ago. What news do you have that prompted the eight a.m. invitation to join you at the temple?"

Brian wasn't prepared for a discussion with Ortiz. He'd hoped to have breakfast and coffee, plan his strategy then meet with the archaeologist at the temple. Seeing no easy way to decline the invitation, Brian sat down. The waiter came and took Brian's order.

"Nothing new, really, except that I want to go with Cory Spencer down into the artifact chamber this morning."

"Certainly. It was my understanding that was what we planned to do today."

"Alone, Dr. Ortiz. Just Cory and me."

Ortiz waved his hand dismissively. "Certainly, senor. No hay probleme." He sipped his coffee.

That was easier than I expected. Too easy, really.

"Dr. Ortiz, what brings you to the hotel so early? Are you meeting Thomas?"

"As a matter of fact I am. He wanted to go over some ideas with me regarding the tests we hope to perform on the metal artifact." Ortiz glanced at his watch. "In fact, he's a little late. That's not like him. He's a very punctual man! I think I'll knock at his door to be sure he's awake."

Dr. Ortiz left the table and walked down the path toward the cabanas. He didn't care if Brian Sadler wanted to go alone into the chamber. At this point Torrance was in charge of decisions and Torrance had instructed the archaeologist to give Brian whatever he wanted. There was no use challenging him – it would only create suspicion.

THE STRANGEST THING

In a few minutes Ortiz walked back through the dining area. Brian glanced at him and Ortiz held up a finger – *back in a minute* – as he strode to the reception lobby.

Ortiz returned to the table and took a seat. "It's puzzling but Mr. Torrance doesn't answer his door. I've asked the clerk to send someone over to check on him. I want to make certain everything is all right."

In less than five minutes the desk clerk walked across the dining patio and told Ortiz that Mr. Torrance's room was empty. Ortiz looked concerned but said nothing.

Something's going on, Brian thought. He attempted to finish his breakfast as nonchalantly as possible. Both men made small talk, each unwilling to discuss the issue that was foremost in his mind.

At 7:45 the FBI agent approached Brian's table. Brian excused himself and left Ortiz finishing coffee. The agent drove directly to the ruins and they walked to the temple. Cory was not in the plaza at the base of the edifice. The men climbed to the rooms at the top. He wasn't there either.

At 8:15 Brian called Dr. Ortiz.

"When do you plan to be at the temple?"

"Do you need me there? I can come now if you wish."

"I need you to unlock the gate to the stairway leading to Pakal's tomb."

"Isn't Cory Spencer there? He usually unlocks it in the morning."

"I don't know where he is. He isn't here."

Ortiz paused. "How strange. I wonder if he and Senor Torrance could be somewhere together. I'll be right over, Senor Sadler."

CHAPTER THIRTY

While Brian Sadler was atop the temple at Palenque, President William Henry Harrison IV signed routine correspondence at his desk in the Oval Office. Around nine a.m. a light on his desk blinked red and Harrison picked up the phone next to it.

"Mr. Sadler's on the line, sir," his personal secretary said. "May I put him through?"

Harry smiled. "Hi, Brian. I hope you have good news for me."

As soon as he heard Brian's voice the President knew something was seriously wrong.

"Harry, something's happened. Thomas Newton Torrance and Cory Spencer are both unaccounted for at the moment. And . . ."

The President interrupted. "Unaccounted for? They're missing?"

"I didn't want to use that word. So far both of them have missed appointments and neither usually does that. But I have something else to tell you too, Harry. About a discovery Cory made here. This is going to blow your mind – it's huge – amazing, Harry. Don't think I've been off smoking the peyote. Everything I'm going to tell you is exactly as I heard it from Cory Spencer last night. And he was scared, Harry. He was terrified of what Torrance might do to take over the discovery that Cory made. He thinks TNT is going to kill him."

"Stop, Brian. Where are you? Are you on a secure line?"

"I'm away from the others, at the temple on my cellphone."

"OK, listen. Tell your FBI agent to take you to a secure place and then use the agent's phone to call me back. I'll be waiting to hear from you."

In ten minutes the men were speaking again. In the Palenque ruins parking lot Brian sat in the embassy's SUV while the agent stood guard outside the vehicle. Brian told President Harrison the entire story he had heard from Cory Spencer.

For the nearly twenty minutes that Brian talked, Harry Harrison said nothing. When the story was finished, the President responded, "So Cory found this hidden passageway around the same time they found the artifact chamber? Is that right? And he kept it secret until he decided to show it to President Chapman?"

"Apparently so. I don't think anybody else knows about it except Torrance. I'm wondering now if he and Torrance went down into the chamber, opened the passage and got trapped inside somehow. If they did, Cory had to have taken Torrance there after he and I talked last night. As scared as he was, I don't believe he would voluntarily take TNT to see the cavern. I wonder if Torrance forced him to go there."

"Have you tried figure out how to open the door to the passageway?"

"Yes. This morning when Cory didn't show up I called Dr. Ortiz, the government archaeologist who's running this project, and got him to open the temple stairway. We went down and looked around the artifact chamber but didn't see anything. I tried for a few minutes to figure out where Cory's two "buttons" were that he pressed to open the door. But Harry, if they're there – if Cory's story is real – they really are just about impossible to find. So far I'm striking out."

"Where was Ortiz while you were trying to find the buttons?"

"He was there with me. The FBI agent won't let me go into the temple alone, and we couldn't force Ortiz to stay at the top, so we all three went down. He asked me why I was pushing around all over the stones at the end of the chamber and I told him I was trying to find something. At that point he let it go but I figure he'll be demanding answers before long."

"Brian, give me an hour or so and I'll call you back on this same phone. I need to get my team together so I can give you direction. Meanwhile, you and the agent go back to the temple. I know you can't keep Dr. Ortiz out of there. But don't let anyone, Ortiz included, go down into that artifact chamber unless you or the FBI agent is with him. If President Chapman's body's there, this is a national security matter, beginning this very minute."

CHAPTER THIRTY-ONE

A million thoughts ran through President Harrison's head. He asked his personal assistant to assemble the national security team in the conference room next door. Then he asked her to get Marianne Chapman on the phone. Nothing was final but he thought as a courtesy he should talk with her himself as soon as possible. This news would travel fast once others found out about it. Leaks were inevitable – it would be bad if the former First Lady heard about this from someone else. When his secretary advised that John Chapman's wife was on the line Harry picked up his phone.

"Marianne, I just wanted to call and give you some information. I don't know yet if this is real or not but we're handling it as though it is."

She interrupted him. "Well hello, *Mister* President," she said, her voice bitter with sarcasm. "I hope you're having a good time sitting in the chair behind the desk where my husband should be." She stifled a sob.

"Marianne, I know this is hard but I need to tell you something . . ."

Her words were slurred. "Oh you know it's hard? How exactly do you know that, Harry? It's not too hard for *you*, is it? *You* run the show now. *Your* wife is the First Lady now. You people should never have rushed to remove John from office. But you were in such a hurry to take the reins yourself." She started crying uncontrollably.

She's drunk, Harry Harrison thought to himself. He glanced at his watch – 10:30 a.m. *Well, she has every right to be with what she's going through.*

She stopped talking as Harry told her only a small part of what he had heard from Brian Sadler. He prefaced his remarks with caution – none of this was confirmed yet. Harry Harrison said that he had been told Chapman's body was in a hidden cavern deep inside the temple he went to Mexico to see. The bite of a poisonous snake was reputed be the cause of death, presuming her husband was in fact deceased. Harrison said nothing about the ancient things that Cory Spencer had allegedly found in the same room.

THE STRANGEST THING

"I'm sorry we don't know any more than this but at least it may be something tangible for the first time since John disappeared."

"That's just great, Harry. Thanks a lot for dropping that news on me. I don't believe a word of what you just said. You can think whatever you wish. I choose to believe he's alive. He's too big an asshole to just die on me. He has to make it harder than that." She sobbed then took a breath.

"I'm sure they're going to find him sitting on a desert island somewhere, bring him back here and you're going to step down and let him have his rightful place back. And I'll have mine too. Is that what you're going to do, Harry? No. Of course it isn't."

She hung up on the President of the United States.

An hour later Harrison's national security team had developed a plan. There were no FBI agents in central Mexico so two CIA operatives from the Embassy in Mexico City were being dispatched to Palenque by private jet. They would arrive this afternoon to assist in the operation.

The Secretary of State placed a call to the Foreign Secretary of Mexico, gave him brief details on what Brian had told them about President Chapman and received permission to do a thorough but again non-invasive search. At this point that was all Harrison wanted – they didn't need to move stones or damage anything. If Cory

Spencer's story were true, they just needed to find two buttons that opened the stone door.

Just before noon Eastern Time the President called Brian back on the FBI agent's phone. The agent answered the call and immediately handed it to Brian, motioning him to step outside on the landing at the top of the Temple of the Inscriptions. Cell service was excellent up this high and Brian needed privacy for this call.

Harrison asked, since they previously spoke, if anyone had attempted to go down the stone staircase into Pakal's tomb. Brian answered negatively. "I've been here the whole time. Dr. Ortiz and the agent have too. We're all at the top. Nobody's gone down the stairs."

"Here's what I need you to do now," he told his old roommate. "Help's on the way, but you and the agent are all we've got for right now. Get down there and figure out how to open that door. I'm sending CIA reinforcements in a couple of hours. I'm hoping you can figure this out fast – before they even get there. I really don't care where Spencer and Torrance are at this point. I just want to know if John Chapman's in there."

CHAPTER THIRTY-TWO

"The agent and I are going back down into the artifact chamber," Brian told Dr. Ortiz after hanging up from the President's call.

"What are you doing, Senor Sadler? Things appear to be getting a little strange. Secret calls. Guarding my temple stairway to keep people out. Feeling the walls and the stone altar in the artifact chamber. What's happening? What are you looking for?"

"Dr. Ortiz, I'm not sure. I'm following orders from the President of the United States and he gave me instructions as to what to do next. I'm not at liberty to tell you what or why. I can't keep you from coming but I could use your help staying up here to make sure no one else comes down. And if you happen to see Cory Spencer or Thomas Newton Torrance I need to know that also."

"I will do as you request for now, Senor Sadler. But let us not forget, I am in charge of this temple and this project. And I will be calling my superiors in Mexico City. You are in our country. Please do not forget that. Our government will tell you what to do, not your presidente.

Brian and the agent walked briskly down the stone steps. *Ortiz had to throw that power thing in. Has to make sure we know who's in charge. Actually I wish I knew what I was doing right now. I have to find these damned indentations.*

The FBI agent with him was accustomed to dealing with information on a need-to-know basis. He kept his mouth shut – at the bottom he said, "If you want me to do anything, Mr. Sadler, all you have to do is ask." Brian asked the agent to remain on the stairs to intercept anyone who might come down. Brian walked around Pakal's sarcophagus and went down the ladder into the room below.

He walked to the far end of the artifact chamber and stood with his right hand on the stone altar. The mangled metal strut lay a foot away from his fingers as they worked their way methodically along the stone. Several times Brian thought he felt a depression – something that might have been Cory's "button" – so he kept a finger on it while he fruitlessly ran his other hand over the wall nearly three feet away. He kept it up for half an hour without success.

THE STRANGEST THING

It's amazing that Cory ever found this at all, Brian thought as he took a break. His arms ached from holding them outstretched.

Back at work, Brian tried combinations of "buttons" time after time to no avail. Since he wasn't sure exactly what he was looking for or what the depressions felt like, this was a daunting task. And there were dozens of natural indentations in the rock wall and the stone altar. The exact two buttons could take weeks to find. Or never be found at all.

Around two p.m. Brian heard noise from the stairway. Someone was coming down. He heard the FBI agent yell, "Halt, I have a weapon!"

Brian climbed the ladder and poked his head into Pakal's tomb chamber. Two men had just reached the bottom of the stone staircase and were standing with their hands up. The agent had his service revolver trained on them. "Whoa!" one shouted. "CIA! Easy, buddy."

"Show me ID," the agent said. "Do it slowly."

The men produced government IDs and the agent holstered his weapon. Brian climbed into the tomb chamber and said, "It's too crowded in here for four people. Let's go upstairs and talk. I've got to get some fresh air and something to drink."

Upstairs, the CIA men introduced themselves and said, "We're to take our instructions from you, Mr. Sadler.

It's my understanding the President has given this the highest priority of national security . . ."

"National security?" Dr. Ortiz asked. "Senor Sadler, I must insist now that you stop whatever you're doing until I can call Mexico City. And you must now tell me what's going on."

Brian started to answer when one of the CIA agents interrupted. He looked at Ortiz coldly. "Sir, you may call whomever you wish. With all respect, we know we are in your country. But we have orders to follow so until someone far, far higher in the pecking order than you tells us differently, Brian can't tell you anything about what's going on here. And he will continue to work in the chamber below. Those are our orders, sir."

"The *pecking order?* No entiendo. *I don't understand.*"

"Dr. Ortiz, you have to give us a little freedom to work right now." Brian sought to assuage his concern. "For now, we have approval through your Foreign Secretary to do non-invasive examination of the artifact chamber. Until that approval is taken away we will move ahead." Sadler knew Ortiz would begin making calls as quickly as he could; he would try to stop things until someone explained what was up. Time could be short and Brian had to find the buttons that opened the door before things became complicated.

After a twenty-minute break and two bottles of water, Brian gave instructions to his newly formed team.

THE STRANGEST THING

He told one of the CIA operatives to remain at the top with Dr. Ortiz. The other would accompany Brian and the FBI man to the chamber. There wasn't much help anyone could give Brian; the search for the buttons was a one-man job given the narrow area in which to stand and the limited places the buttons conceivably could be. But he wanted people from the U.S. government with him in case he succeeded in opening the door.

Ortiz had been on the phone most of the time Brian was on break. He had talked quietly in Spanish but apparently had no success in convincing anyone to countermand the Foreign Secretary's order from earlier today. At least so far.

"OK, let's go," Brian said.

Ortiz walked to the stairway. "This time I go with you. You have a man here to watch the staircase and guard against intruders. This time I will see what you are doing."

The room couldn't easily hold four people and Brian had no authority to order Ortiz to stay away. Reluctantly he left the second CIA man at the top as well.

In the artifact chamber Brian resumed the boring, mindless work of running his fingers a centimeter at a time over and over the surface of the rock to his right, finding something that might work then running his left hand up and down the rock wall.

Nothing.

Dr. Ortiz watched intently. Several times he took pictures with his phone. Brian watched him. He knew Ortiz would send those to his superiors to support his request to stop Brian's examination.

About an hour was all Brian could do at one stretch. The tension from holding his hands out for such a long time was exhausting. His muscles ached but he wanted to keep going – there was no way to tell how much time he had left before Dr. Ortiz would successfully stop his efforts. So long as Ortiz was in the chamber with Brian, the archaeologist's phone couldn't receive a call – there was no signal this deep in the temple. So Brian pushed on, straining his arms and slowly feeling every indentation.

By three p.m. Brian had easily checked a thousand little depressions, and probably had gone over a lot of them more than once. But he had kept going. He had been doing this for hours and he was physically drained. He gave himself until three-thirty. He would have to quit then. Once he stopped he was certain Ortiz would get the project put on hold. That would mean Brian had failed the President. He would have failed to complete the search for President Chapman.

At ten minutes after three Brian put his fingers on an indentation in the stone altar and another on the stone wall. He pressed. The same way he had pressed over and over all day long.

Without a sound the door swung open.

CHAPTER THIRTY-THREE

The men in the chamber gave a collective shout of surprise. Since the only activity was watching Brian methodically move his fingers around, Dr. Ortiz had almost fallen asleep and the FBI agent was struggling not to join him. The air was stuffy and hot; Brian's muscles ached so when the stone quietly moved back into the passageway they all jumped at once.

"Santa Madre de Dios!" Ortiz yelled. *Holy Mother of God!*

The agent moved next to Brian, his pistol drawn and ready for whatever might lie in the darkness ahead. But there were no sounds from the corridor.

"How many flashlights do we have?" Brian asked.

There were two among the three of them – only the agent didn't have a light. "I'll stay with you," he told

Brian. "Let me go first – you hold the light and shine it in front of me."

Ortiz brought up the rear. The three started down the corridor, pausing a moment at the first glyph on the wall. Ortiz looked at it, puzzled at what it could mean, but he hurried ahead when the other two men continued walking. Brian had no time to look at the things Cory Spencer had described. His job was to find President Chapman.

Brian shone the light on the second hieroglyph and Ortiz glanced at it while he walked on down the chamber. They arrived at the large cavern. Brian directed his light toward the center of the room. A mass of metal lay roughly in the middle, as he had been prepared to expect, and a body was visible on the ground. He ran to it. "It's President Chapman," he said, anticipating.

But it wasn't Chapman. Brian turned the body over and looked into the face of Cory Spencer. Blood covered the front of his shirt. As Brian touched his neck to feel for a pulse, Spencer's eyes opened.

"Brian," he said weakly. "You've come. Thank God. President Chapman's body is over there." He pointed an unsteady hand to his left. The beam of Brian's light caught the second man's body.

The FBI agent grabbed Ortiz's flashlight and shone it in Chapman's face. "Mr. Sadler, I can go up to the top and notify my office if you want . . ."

THE STRANGEST THING

"I'll handle it. The President told me to call him personally. I need to wait a minute, though. There's one more thing – Cory, do you have any idea where Thomas Torrance is?"

"Yes," Cory struggled to answer. "He shot me, then . . . then he fell into the metal thing. I remember seeing little sparks right before he fell in. Don't touch anything in there . . ."

"He *shot* you?"

Cory was too weak to respond.

"Keep your gun out, just in case," Brian told the FBI agent. He looked inside the oval object. There were no sparks and no body - nothing at all but a group of dusty gray capsule-like things, each about eight inches long.

"He's not in here. Do you know if there's another way out of this cavern?"

"I have no idea," Spencer slurred. He closed his eyes and his body slumped.

"Stay awake, Cory! Don't leave me now!"

"I'm just so tired . . ." he responded, his voice barely a whisper.

"We're going to get help for you. Right now."

Brian formulated a quick plan. He left the armed FBI agent with Cory in case Torrance was hiding nearby. Then he asked Dr. Ortiz to remain in Pakal's tomb at the bottom of the stone staircase. That was to ensure no one else came in or out of the passageway.

At the top of the temple Brian pulled out his phone. He needed help quickly and thought it would be fastest to work through the Embassy. He clicked on the number.

"Cultural Affairs," a pleasant voice answered.

"This is an emergency," Brian said. "Give me the Ambassador's office. Now!"

The call was transferred and within two minutes an administrative assistant had put Brian on hold while she located the Ambassador.

"Mr. Sadler. Good afternoon. What can I do for you?"

Brian spent only a moment filling the diplomat in on the shooting of an American citizen at the ruin. "I don't have time to figure all this out. The President's Gulfstream's here and we can get the archaeologist out but I need medical attention for him fast. He's going to die if we don't get it."

"I'll call you back in five minutes." The Ambassador was fully aware that Brian Sadler was operating with the authority of the President of the

THE STRANGEST THING

United States and he moved quickly. His assistant called the small local hospital in Palenque and made preparations for the arrival of a gunshot patient. The Federal Police would be notified by the hospital; the Ambassador would smooth things with them as soon as the patient arrived.

He called Brian and told him to move Cory by car to the Palenque hospital. "I'll work on getting him to Mexico City to a major trauma center – I'll ask the President to authorize the Gulfstream."

"No need," Brian replied. "I have authority to instruct the pilots to fly to Mexico City. I'll take care of that as soon as Cory's stabilized in the local facility here. Thanks for your help."

While Brian made arrangements for Cory's medical treatment Dr. Ortiz and the three government men down below devised a makeshift plan to move Cory. Using a bed sheet they retrieved from the crew bunkhouse the four men carried the archaeologist out of the cavern, hoisted him up the ladder then did the best they could on the narrow stairs. Brian instructed one of the CIA agents to take Cory to the hospital in the SUV. After a brief examination and efforts to stabilize him, Cory was taken by air ambulance from Palenque to Mexico City, kept in the hospital overnight then flown to New York.

Once the immediate need to help Cory was dealt with, Dr. Ortiz called in the Federal Police to secure the Temple of the Inscriptions. With Torrance unaccounted for there was a chance he could reappear at any time. He had shot Cory Spencer – he was considered armed and dangerous.

Brian called President Harrison who put the call on speakerphone after bringing his Chief of Staff into the room. Brian reported that Chapman's body had been found just as Cory Spencer had said it would. Then he outlined the rest of what he knew – after shooting Cory, Thomas Newton Torrance had apparently fallen into the oval egg-like object but was nowhere to be found now. He described the glyphs and the mysterious artifacts in the cavern. The President and Bob Parker listened intently until Brian was finished, then Harry Harrison told Brian what would happen next. They had been working on a plan since Brian's earlier call today that Chapman's body might be in the temple.

Instead of being used to fly Brian home from Palenque, the Gulfstream brought the body of former President John Chapman back to Andrews Air Force Base where a toxicology report confirmed the cause of death as poisoning by the bite of a fer-de-lance. Shortly the nation focused on President Chapman's upcoming funeral in Washington.

CHAPTER THIRTY-FOUR
The Aftermath

Marianne Chapman did not attend her husband's funeral. Immediately following her last conversation with President Harrison she had taken an overdose of barbiturates. She was found the next morning by the Secret Service agent assigned to protect her. The day of John Chapman's funeral was the fourth day she had been in a coma. She would recover from this episode but within a year she tried again. This time it worked. She died at the age of fifty-five and was buried in her hometown of Omaha, Nebraska.

Thomas Newton Torrance was gone. His pistol and cellphone lay inside the oval metal object into which Cory said he had fallen. The gun and phone were nestled amid the small capsule things. Government agents who were careful not to touch the ancient objects carefully retrieved them. The phone was slightly radioactive and,

231

perplexingly, it remained fully charged after nearly twenty hours without external power. The gun bore the fingerprints of Thomas Newton Torrance. One bullet had been fired - that shell casing was retrieved from the floor of the cavern. That bullet had entered and exited the body of Cory Spencer.

The Sussex University dig supervisor was recovering at Lenox Hill Hospital in Manhattan. Shot once in the gut with a .38 caliber bullet, Cory had lain in the cavern roughly fifteen hours before Brian Sadler successfully determined how to open the door and find him. He lost a lot of blood but was expected to make a full recovery. Caroline Tipton, his old lover and benefactor, was by his side in the hospital every day.

Ultimately Thomas Newton Torrance was proven correct in his assessment about Cory Spencer's discovery of what appeared to be an extraterrestrial craft. The scientific community discounted it completely, calling it an elaborate hoax. Senior academicians at Sussex University pulled Cory aside and advised him to stop talking about it. The implication was that Cory's future as an archaeologist was in jeopardy so long as he continued to rant and rave about aliens. At least for now Cory Spencer wasn't becoming famous as a result of the most amazing discovery in the world. He was saying nothing about it.

In hopes of finding the way Torrance escaped, both the American and Mexican authorities carefully examined every inch of the artifact chamber, the cavern and the passageway between the two. Although several side caves and short dead-end passages were found, there were no more artifacts and no sign of the British entrepreneur. He had vanished.

Ancient astronaut theorists were having a field day – for them there finally was proof that aliens have visited our planet. For now nobody could come up with a rational, levelheaded scientific idea what the things were or what the glyphs meant. History International and Discovery were already sparring to win the contract for exclusive broadcast rights. This drama would unfold over years, not days or months, but each network wanted to be a part of it every step of the way. This would be one of the biggest stories ever. Every fan of the books of Erich von Daniken, Graham Hancock or David Hatcher Childress would be in seventh heaven. This was exciting for those who believed that others had visited Earth.

On the scientific side, a team of experts was already being assembled to examine the discovery in the cavern below King Pakal's tomb. They would look at the metal strut the team originally found, the glyphs, the two "egg pod" pieces and the capsule things inside the pods. No one would speculate whether a reasonable explanation would ever be forthcoming. This was just too bizarre, too different and unusual.

As the financier and benefactor of the Palenque project, Thomas Newton Torrance should have had significant input into how all this played out but he was nowhere to be found. He had no direct heirs and his executor was his old mentor from the early days of TNT's wheeling and dealing.

But was Torrance dead? Nobody knew. To further complicate things, the man had been residing in the USA, was a citizen of the UK and went missing in Mexico. In the USA and the UK a missing person can be declared dead by a court after seven years. The law in Mexico wasn't as clear.

A warrant was issued for his arrest on a charge of attempted murder but Thomas Newton Torrance would never be found. It would take years and many court battles before he was declared dead and his affairs wound up. Notwithstanding the ten million dollars he had put into the Palenque project and despite the incredible discovery there, Torrance's estate did not profit from it, nor was he given credit as a discoverer. Cory Spencer sued the estate for a portion of the proceeds and a court awarded him a million dollars.

Dr. Ortiz had profited by more than twenty thousand dollars thanks to the cash TNT provided him in exchange for information. Ortiz dreamed he might become the next Zahi Hawass — like the famous Egyptian archaeologist, Ortiz believed he could emerge as the spokesperson for archaeology all over Mexico and Central America. Sadly, without either the personality or connections of Dr. Hawass, Ortiz was destined to fade into history. He was noted as having been present when the artifacts were found but his negligible contribution was not considered meaningful. He started a book about the discoveries at Palenque but never finished it.

THE STRANGEST THING

At the President's request Brian stayed on site at Palenque for several days after Chapman's body was removed, acting as a representative of the U.S. government. Sussex University issued a recall for its remaining team members after the Mexican authorities revoked its permit to dig. The Mexican government would henceforth manage further exploration of the artifact chamber, cavern and the mysterious objects. For the moment everything was halted and the Temple of the Inscriptions remained closed to the public.

Because Harry Harrison asked Brian to remain in Palenque the plans for a trip to Cancun had to be cancelled. "We'll get it done, Nicole," he had said after she expressed her disappointment. "Just give me a little time and we'll do it right."

Two weeks later Brian Sadler and Nicole Farber were invited to the White House for a private dinner with the Harrisons. They declined. "Give us a rain check, Harry," Brian had told his old roommate. "We have a side trip to take first."

Three weeks after the events in Palenque Nicole and Brian sat on lounge chairs in the sun. They had carved out the time for their trip to Cancun and now sat on a sandy beach ten feet from the ocean. They were at Manana Beach Resort on the Playa del Carmen, the place Nicole had picked out for them. A gentle breeze blew and waves cascaded into shore with a soothing sound. It was as peaceful and calming as either of them could imagine.

A waiter came by and they ordered another round of Margaritas. "It's getting easier," Nicole said lazily.

"What's getting easier?"

"It's getting easier to sit here naked and order drinks from a waiter. I have to tell you, I had a little concern whether I could do this. I wondered if the waiter would look me over while I placed my order. And sure enough, he does! But I think it's the most exhilarating thing I've ever experienced. I feel free! It's so much fun not to have any clothes on!"

"And you can get a tan with no tan lines."

"Yep. That too. So can you. Don't burn anything I might need later." She smiled at him mischievously.

"Dinner's at seven. What are you wearing? The black outfit or the blue one?"

Nicole smiled and thought for a moment. "I think I'll wear the fleshtone outfit. I know you've seen me in it a lot the last couple of days but I like it."

"Damn right. I like it too. It's the best outfit you have!"

"This old thing? It's been around awhile." She lay back in the lounge chair and ran her hand up and down her leg.

"Not nearly long enough for me." Brian leaned over and kissed her. Her nipple brushed against his arm and he kissed her again, more deeply.

She glanced at him. "Better be careful raising that flagpole out here on the beach, Mister Sadler!"

So they decided to take a break and run back up to their suite. That interlude lasted all afternoon and ended with a dip in the Jacuzzi situated in their bedroom by the front door. They opened the curtains and the sliding doors so they could lounge in the tub and watch the ocean. People walked by on the sidewalk ten feet in front of their room but took no notice of their nudity. Of course they didn't – this was Manana Beach, after all.

Later they sat in the dining room and sipped martinis as they perused the menu. They laughed at how different it felt to be in traditional social settings such as a dining room full of other couples with no one wearing anything at all.

During their vacation they spent long hours talking through their situation. Nothing long-term was worked out. Brian couldn't move and neither could Nicole. When they were together they were as close as two people could be. And they vowed to keep the spark alive when they were apart. Even though the "see other people" plan was still in place, Brian just wanted to see more of this one.

EPILOGUE

Sixty-five million years ago an asteroid six miles in diameter, the size of a small town, slammed into what is now the Yucatan Peninsula of Mexico. Travelling tens of thousands of miles an hour, it was possibly the most catastrophic impact the earth ever experienced and it left a crater over a hundred miles wide. The force of the collision caused dramatic changes on our planet.

Massive volumes of ash and smoke erupted into the atmosphere of the earth and mega-tsunamis engulfed much of the land. Scientists theorize that the abrupt extinction of the dinosaurs happened because of this event. Most of those creatures, the remains of which were often found with food still in their stomachs, died suddenly. Many experts believe this asteroid impact is the reason.

For perhaps a decade the skies of the entire planet were covered with a blanket of ash. Almost no plants or animals survived. Evolutionists think the ones that did, the smallest of species, arose from the ashes and ultimately repopulated Earth, resulting in the plethora of living things we know today.

There was one other species on our planet when the asteroid struck. Fifteen of these creatures were here – close to the Yucatan, less than three hundred miles from the impact site. They were the most intelligent things on Earth at the time the cataclysm occurred. Others of their type watched helplessly from ten thousand miles above the planet as their compatriots calmly gathered in the pod that had brought them to Earth. They had no emotions – there was no sorrow, no grief. They merely registered the loss of their fellow beings when the catastrophe happened.

For years these creatures had struggled in vain to restart the propulsion device on the craft that might have taken them off the planet. But they had crash-landed only a few hundred years ago in Earth-time. After numerous attempts the creatures had failed to get the oval spacecraft repaired. One of the struts had been ripped off the vehicle and severely damaged in the crash and the beings could not reattach it. Without the fourth strut the propulsion mechanism would not generate power because the craft had to be level for its sophisticated systems to start.

The strut was made from the strongest, densest metal in the universe. Similar to iridium, it had not previously been seen on Earth. Due to its density the eight-foot-long strut weighed nearly ten thousand pounds.

Once they gave up trying to reattach the strut, the tiny capsule-like beings moved it out of their way to a stone altar they constructed using the technique of levitation. Multi-ton rocks moved where the beings directed them, without the use of tools. Same for the strut itself. They merely raised it into the air and shifted it over to the altar.

The creatures also created two glyphs in the walls of a passageway leading from the large area where their craft lay. One glyph depicted the fifteen beings and their spacecraft. The other was intended to tell others in the future where they had come from – a binary star system four light years, or twenty-four trillion miles, away from Earth.

The twenty-foot long egg-shaped vehicle, which had reliably brought these small beings to our solar system and the third planet from the sun, had started its journey on a planet orbiting the double star Alpha Centauri. Its system had fifteen planets and theirs was fourth from their binary sun. Their craft had traveled for nearly two thousand years. The goal was to reach our solar system and to investigate whether it had a planet that could support their form of life. Nothing was wrong with the place from which they had come. It was merely logic that required the creatures to plan for every possible outcome. Their requirements for a new home were few – primarily they required a temperate climate free from poisons and caustic chemicals in the atmosphere. Earth turned out to be the perfect place.

The creatures were far different from the plants and animals that would eventually populate Earth. They were alive in one sense of the word but they were not living things. They were eight-inch long sophisticated machines with artificial intelligence – they were computers that looked like little capsules. Each one had four antennae with knobs on the ends – those resembled hands and feet but they had a different use - they mined data for the beings.

After Earth's impact with the asteroid the creatures that had watched the scene from space returned to the Alpha Centauri system. They knew it would be a very long time before this green planet could again be of use to them. The atmosphere had to clear. The climate had to warm up.

This advanced civilization of machines had no measure of time – they simply had no use for the concept. Therefore they waited to revisit Earth until it was necessary. At last their planet began to lose its mild climate. The huge double suns pulsated from time to time. As the fluctuations became more frequent the planet these robotic creatures inhabited began to warm. Soon it would be too hot for their sophisticated circuitry. These machines sent another mission to Earth. The goal was to determine if the planet was ready for them.

Sixty-five million years had passed since the previous group of these beings had lain dormant on the earth during the asteroid cataclysm. The second mission arrived around 5000 B.C. as people on Earth measured time. It returned to the site of the previous crash and hovered several miles above the planet.

The place where the ship had crashed was now covered. Ash and debris from the asteroid impact had solidified to form caves. The ruined spacecraft that held fifteen of their fellow creatures was now in an underground cavern.

The beings noted much activity on the planet. It was different than their last visit when enormous dinosaurs roamed the forests. Their imaging systems showed that a variety of things lived here – plants, animals, even humans. Although they had never previously encountered the species homo sapiens, they quickly determined these creatures that walked upright on two appendages were apparently the most intelligent things on the planet. That wasn't saying much - the level of logical thinking of which these machine creatures were capable was exponentially greater than that of the human beings.

Egyptians, the Aztec, Maya and Incas, and others around the world - the people who built massive structures – pyramids, temples, multi-story buildings, virtual skyscrapers – learned those techniques from these interplanetary travelers. They were taught principles of construction, basic physics and geometry and mathematics. They mastered astronomy and strange things like levitation, hypnotism and mummification.

The beings spent over six thousand years on Earth during their second visit. Their time here stretched from the building of the pyramids in Egypt to the middle of the sixteenth century A.D. Then it was time to return to their solar system, to advise their people that Earth was ready for colonization. Around 1550 as humans measure time, they left for the four thousand year round trip to Alpha Centauri.

The craft that had crashed sixty-five million years ago remained hidden in the jungles of what is now southern Mexico. It contained fifteen beings – fifteen little capsules.

Until Thomas Newton Torrance fell into the pod, that is. Now there were sixteen.